Dear Reader,

I'm often asked how I got my start as a writer. When I tell them that my first novels were romances for Bantam's Loveswept line, they're often surprised. Although this genre may seem as though it's quite different from the suspense I now write, the two have more in common than it seems.

For me, every good story has two essential elements: characters to fall in love with and a mystery to be solved—whether it's an unsolved crime or that complex emotion that bewilders us most of all: love. Even the most sophisticated murder plot can't compare to the perplexing inner mechanisms of the human heart.

In *Rumor Has It,* Katie Quaid meets Nick Leone, a Yankee heartthrob with a mysterious past and a rogue's smile that seems to dare Katie to unmask him. The proper Southern lady has her own deep secrets and, for years, has buried herself in her work, restoring historic homes, while trying to recover from an accident that destroyed a lifelong dream. Nick vows to melt the walls of the woman others call an ice princess. Will they be able to build a love that bridges two different dreams?

I loved writing about Katie and Nick's journey years ago, and hope that you'll enjoy it today.

All my best,

Tami Hoag

Tami Hoag

Praise for the Bestsellers of Tami Hoag

THE ALIBI MAN

"Captivating thriller ... [Elena] is a heroine readers will want to see more of." —*Publishers Weekly*

"Hard to put down." —*Washington Post*

"A superbly taut thriller. Written in a staccato style that will have readers racing through the pages ... Will leave readers breathless and satisfied." —*Booklist*

"A suspenseful tale, with a surprising ending; the author once again has constructed a hard-hitting story with interesting characters and a thrilling plot." —*Midwest Book Review*

"Elena Estes [is] one of Hoag's most complicated, difficult and intriguing characters.... Hoag enhances a tight mystery plot with an over-the-shoulder view of the Palm Beach polo scene, giving her readers an up-close-and-personal look at the rich and famous.... *The Alibi Man* is her best work to date." —BookReporter.com

"An engrossing story and a cast of well-drawn characters." —*Minneapolis Star Tribune*

"[Hoag] gets better with every book. One of the tautest thrillers I have read for a long while." —*Bookseller* (UK)

"Hoag certainly knows how to build a plot and her skill has deservedly landed her on bestseller lists numerous times." —*South Florida Sun-Sentinel*

"Hoag has a winner in this novel where she brings back Elena Estes.... Hoag is the consummate story-teller and creator of suspense." —*Mystery News*

"Tami Hoag weaves an intricate tale of murder and deception.... A very well-written and thought-out murder/mystery. Hoag is able to keep you guessing and you'll be left breathless until all the threads are unwoven and the killer is revealed." —*FreshFiction.com*

PRIOR BAD ACTS

"A snappy, scary thriller." —*Entertainment Weekly*

"Stunning... Here [Hoag] stands above the competition, creating complex characters who evolve more than those in most thrillers. The breathtaking plot twists are perfectly paced in this compulsive page-turner." —*Publishers Weekly* (starred review)

"A chilling thriller with a romantic chaser."
—*New York Daily News*

"A first-rate thriller with an ending that will knock your socks off." —*Booklist*

"An engrossing thriller with plenty of plot twists and a surprise ending." —*OK!* magazine

"A chilling tale of murder and mayhem." —*BookPage*

"The in-depth characterization and the unrelenting suspense are what makes *Prior Bad Acts* an outstanding read. Gritty and brutal at times, *Prior Bad Acts* de-

livers a stunning novel of murder, vengeance and retribution.... Riveting and chilling suspense."
—*Romance Reviews Today*

KILL THE MESSENGER

"Excellent pacing and an energetic plot heighten the suspense.... Enjoyable." —*Chicago Tribune*

"Everything rings true, from the zippy cop-shop banter, to the rebellious bike messenger subculture, to the ultimate, heady collision of Hollywood money, politics, and power." —*Minneapolis Star Tribune*

"Hoag's usual crisp, uncluttered storytelling and her ability to make us care about her characters triumph in *Kill the Messenger*." —*Fort Lauderdale Sun-Sentinel*

"A perfect book. It is well written, and it has everything a reader could hope for.... It cannot be put down.... Please don't miss this one." —*Kingston (MA) Observer*

"[A] brisk read...it demonstrates once again why [Hoag's] so good at what she does."
—*San Francisco Chronicle*

"Action-filled ride...a colorful, fast-paced novel that will keep you guessing." —*Commercial Appeal*

"High-octane suspense...Nonstop action moves the story forward at a breath-stealing pace, and the tension remains high from beginning to end.... Suspense at its very best." —*Romance Reviews Today*

"Hoag's loyal readers and fans of police procedural suspense novels will definitely love it." —*Booklist*

"*Kill the Messenger* will add to [Hoag's] list of winners.... This is a fast-moving thriller with a great plot and wonderful characters. The identity of the killer is a real surprise." —*Somerset (PA) Daily American*

"Engaging...the triumph of substance over style... character-driven, solidly constructed thriller."
—*Publishers Weekly*

"Hoag upholds her reputation as one of the hottest writers in the suspense genre with this book, which not only has a highly complex mystery, multilayered suspense and serpentine plot, but also great characterizations...an entertaining and expertly crafted novel not to be missed." —*CurledUp.com*

DARK HORSE

"A thriller as tightly wound as its heroine...Hoag has created a winning central figure in Elena....Bottom line: Great ride." —*People*

"This is her best to date.... [A] tautly told thriller."
—*Minneapolis Star Tribune*

"Hoag proves once again why she is considered a queen of the crime thriller."
—*Charleston (SC) Post & Courier*

"A tangled web of deceit and double-dealing makes for a fascinating look into the wealthy world of horses juxtaposed with the realistic introspection of one very troubled ex-cop. A definite winner." —*Booklist*

"Anyone who reads suspense novels regularly is acquainted with Hoag's work—or certainly should be. She's one of the most consistently superior suspense and romantic suspense writers on today's bestseller lists. A word of warning to readers: don't think you know whodunit 'til the very end." —*Clute (TX) Facts*

"Suspense, shocking violence, and a rip-roaring conclusion—this novel has all the pulse-racing touches that put Tami Hoag books on bestseller lists and crime fans' reading lists." —*Baton Rouge Advocate Magazine*

"Full of intrigue, glitter, and skullduggery... [Hoag] is a master of suspense." —*Publishers Weekly*

"Her best to date, an enjoyable read, and a portent of even better things to come." —*Grand Rapids Press*

"A complex cerebral puzzle that will keep readers on the edge until all the answers are revealed."
—*Midwest Book Review*

"To say that Tami Hoag is the absolute best at what she does is a bit easy since she is really the only person who does what she does.... It is a testament to Hoag's skill that she is able to go beyond being skillful and find the battered hearts in her characters, and capture their beating on the page.... A superb read."
—*Detroit News & Free Press*

TAMI HOAG

Rumor Has It

BANTAM BOOKS

RUMOR HAS IT
A Bantam Book

PUBLISHING HISTORY
Loveswept edition published January 1989
Bantam mass market edition / February 2009

Published by Bantam Dell
A Division of Random House, Inc.
New York, New York

This is a work of fiction. Names, characters, places, and incidents
either are the product of the author's imagination or are used
fictitiously. Any resemblance to actual persons, living or dead,
events, or locales is entirely coincidental.

Bantam Books and the rooster colophon are registered trademarks
of Random House, Inc.

ISBN 978-0-553-59231-3

Printed in the United States of America
Published simultaneously in Canada

www.bantamdell.com

OPM   10 9 8 7 6 5 4 3 2 1

Rumor Has It

ONE

"HE CAN'T BE single," Mary Margaret McSwain said, adjusting the focus on her binoculars as she peered at the store across the street. "He's too good-looking. It's McSwain's Law: If a man's gorgeous, he has to be married, gay, or a serial killer."

Zoe Baylor shoved a book of wallpaper samples out of her way and leaned across the oak table, bracing her long dark hands against the window frame as she tried to get a better look without benefit of magnifying lenses.

"Mary Margaret," Katie Quaid called in a

warning tone as she struggled in the back door of the store, her tiny frame weaving under the weight of books of drapery swatches. After the day she'd had, she wouldn't have refused a hand, but her friends seemed too preoccupied to offer. "I don't want to hear another one of your stories about serial killers. Mrs. Pruitt changed her mind again about the color of the guest room. If you describe to me one more brutal way to do away with somebody, no one is liable to find Mrs. Pruitt for a long, long time."

Katie dropped the drapery samples on her desk with a horrendous crash. Neither of the women staring out the window so much as flinched. The tip of Zoe's nose dotted the plate glass in front of her like that of a hungry kid looking in a bakery window. Katie's business partner, known as Maggie to her friends, was kneeling on her chair, her well-rounded bottom sticking up as she leveled a pair of binoculars at some point across the street.

"Maggie, what on earth are you doing?" Katie asked. She knew her friend already had a solidly established reputation for being a flake. Spying on people with binoculars was not going to improve matters.

"I'm spying on the Adonis in the store across the street." Maggie sighed and moaned, never lowering her binoculars. "Haven't you heard? That old building was sold two days ago."

"Who bought it?"

Maggie sat back with her legs tucked under her and offered the binoculars to Katie, deftly untangling the neck strap from the ends of her bobbed red hair. The smile that tilted her mouth was challenging. "See for yourself."

Katie rolled her eyes and propped a fist on her slender hip. "I will not stoop to window peeping."

"Chicken."

Muttering under her breath, Katie grabbed the field glasses from her friend and raised them to her eyes. Would she always be such a sucker for a dare? Probably. It had something to do with being only five feet one and seven-eighths inches tall. Being the first one to take a dare had always been her way of compensating for her lack of stature. That she was twenty-seven and had long since considered herself a grown woman had no effect on the trait.

"If this isn't the silliest thing you've..." The rest of her breath washed out of her on the softest of sighs as she focused the binoculars.

The dark T-shirt might have been painted on him. Even looking through the window of her store and the bay window of the store across the street, Katie could see the outline of his chest muscles, a wide expanse of hard, rippling pectorals. He was dancing as he washed the inside of the window. His breathtaking chest tapered to a narrow waist, and then to hips that were gently gyrating in time to the tune he was listening to on his headphones. He had the kind of body that was made for faded jeans—a flat belly, a perfectly rounded male fanny, slim hips, and muscular thighs.

Before Katie could dwell on any other part of his lower anatomy, she jerked the glasses up to his face. She might have lost her breath again, except she hadn't been breathing. Inky black hair tumbled onto his forehead, lending his male beauty a roguish quality. Maggie hadn't been far wrong calling him an Adonis. His was the kind of face ancient Greek sculptors would have fought over to immortalize in marble.

"His name is *Nick Leone*," Maggie said, as if it were the most dangerously mysterious name she'd ever heard. "He's from *New Jersey*. Lee Henry Bartell heard it from Dee Roberts, the real estate agent who sold him the property."

"What's he doing in Briarwood?" Zoe asked suspiciously. In a nervous habit she ran a forefinger back and forth over the plastic name tag on her nurse's uniform.

Katie forced herself to plunk the binoculars down on the table, embarrassed over her own involuntary reaction to the handsome stranger. She was no drooling man watcher; she had a business to run. "He must not know about the law against people from New Jersey moving to Virginia," she said in a teasing voice.

Zoe was too wrapped up in her musings to hear. "I thought he sounded like a Yankee," she murmured.

Maggie jumped on the comment like a cat on a june bug. "You heard him talk? You met him? Where? What's he like? He doesn't have a funny voice, does he? That would just ruin it for me if he had a funny voice. Where'd you see him?"

A horrified look came over Zoe's long, thin face. "Nowhere."

"The hospital." Maggie nodded, her brown eyes narrowing in thought. "Hmmm, that's interesting. What was he there for?"

"Maggie!" Zoe exclaimed. "You know I can't talk about patients. It's not ethical."

"And it's none of your business, Mary Margaret," Katie added pointedly. "Have you called in the order for that grass paper John Harris wants in his office?"

"Yes. You know what the rumor is about him?"

"I don't want to hear any rumors about John Harris," Katie said, deliberately misinterpreting Maggie's question. She had a feeling the less she knew about the gorgeous arrangement of masculinity across the street, the better off she'd be. She scooped a couple of wallpaper books off the long table and returned them to their proper slots in the oak case along the wall.

"Not John Harris, Nick Leone!"

"Lord, Mary Margaret, the man hasn't been in town a week, and already there's gossip about him?" Katie pulled out a book of miniature country prints and headed for her desk. "I wonder if he knows what he's in for, moving to a small town."

"Rumor has it he's a *mole*." She raised her carefully plucked eyebrows for emphasis.

Katie ignored her, sitting down to page through the book, concentrating on paisley prints in order to get her mind off perfect male pectorals. Zoe shrugged. "I don't get it."

Maggie heaved a sigh. "A spy for the Company, an agent for the CIA. You know, double O, licensed to kill. They're called moles. Don't you ever go to the movies?"

"The CIA," Zoe whispered, rubbing her name tag. "I heard he was a fashion model."

"Oh, please," Katie said, laughing at her friends' wild imaginations. "I don't know which one of you is worse. Maggie, how can you make such a ridiculous remark?"

"I'm only telling you what I heard, sugar. Lee Henry told me that Dee said the man was very reluctant to discuss himself, and when she asked him what he used to do up in New Jersey, he wouldn't exactly say."

"That's all?" Katie questioned, trying to suppress a grin. "Lee Henry didn't see him talking into the secret phone in the heel of his shoe?"

Zoe muttered to herself, "So that's how he came by that gunshot wound."

"Gunshot wound!" Maggie bolted out of her chair to lean across the table and over her friend.

"Oh, damn! Don't tell anyone I told you!"

"A gunshot wound. What do you have to say about that, Katie Quaid?"

Katie wouldn't have shown her surprise at the news for anything. She kept her eyes glued to the flowered paper in front of her. "He was probably shot by some flighty woman who heard a wild rumor he was a secret agent. Maybe he had a hunting accident. Maybe he's a retired police officer. Maybe—"

"—we should find out for ourselves," Maggie interrupted smoothly, lifting the binoculars to her eyes again. She zoomed them in on Katie. "I'm leaning toward the story that he's in the federal witness-protection program. But in the interest of truth, I vote Katie our official ambassador and spy."

"I second," Zoe said, nodding enthusiastically as she caught Maggie's wink.

"Nominations cease. Go check him out, Katie."

"Don't be absurd." She shot Maggie a look from beneath lowered brows. They had been friends since their freshman year at William and Mary. Katie had no doubt that Maggie had caught her automatic response to Nick Leone and had decided to exercise her self-appointed role of fairy godmother.

"What? Are you scared? Do you secretly believe he's a double agent?" Maggie asked, pushing all the right buttons inside Katie without the slightest compunction. "I dare you to go find out."

Nick was happily lost in thought as he washed the dirt off the panes of the bay window. Wash, rinse, polish dry, move a little to the tunes from his favorite musical group—what a great life. Not many guys thirty-two years old were able to say they were living out one of their life dreams. He hadn't made it big on Broadway—that had been his first dream—but he'd given it his best shot. His second dream had been to start his own restaurant in a small, quiet town. He'd signed the papers on the beginning of that dream two days ago.

A lot of people thought he was nuts. His friends back home had been sure he would be massacred by wild men if he moved to Virginia. They had seemed genuinely uncertain as to whether Briarwood, Virginia, had as yet benefited from electricity and indoor plumbing.

As far as Nick was concerned, Briarwood had it all over any big city. He had been born and raised in Atlantic City and had spent much of his adult life in New York City, but in his heart he always had thought of himself as a small-town boy. The performer in him had yearned for bright lights, but offstage he had found cities could be lonely, unfriendly, dangerous—he rubbed his healing shoulder—places. His friends could have the dirty gray streets, the crime, the garbage-haulers' strikes, the pollution. He would take a nice quiet life in a town where people didn't need five locks on their front door.

Nick had seen for himself how friendly the people in the small town were. Everyone said hello to him on the street. They were talkative—slow talkers compared to those he was used to, but they liked to talk. You couldn't buy a candy bar without having to tell at least one person your whole life story.

A frown creased his brow at this thought. He had evaded their questions as politely as he could. Nick had a feeling the people in the conservative rural community wouldn't understand if he were to tell them what he'd spent the last two years doing.

"Pardon me," Katie said, stepping through the open front door. He went on polishing the glass in the bay window, his hips swaying seductively. The blue foam pads of his headphones pressed against his ears. They were very nicely shaped ears, she noticed. Her stomach tightened. Immediately she began to scold herself. She wasn't at all a nervous person, and she simply did not ever allow herself to go gaga over a man. There was no point in it. Not even if the small of his back was the sexiest thing she'd ever seen wrapped in a skintight T-shirt.

Squelching her jitters, Katie crossed to where he was standing and pulled the plug on his music, disconnecting the cord that ran from the head-phones into the tiny cassette player that was hooked onto his waistband.

Suddenly Nick's head swung in her direction. She took an involuntary step back as she felt the impact of his gaze. His eyes were brown—a rich coffee brown that darkened to chocolate as he looked at her. His grin was engaging, endearingly crooked, giving a boyish quality to his classic good looks. He pulled the headphones down around his neck.

"Are you the welcome-wagon lady?" he asked, his gaze shifting to the bouquet of spring flowers in a china vase she clutched before her. Someone should have captured her on canvas, he thought. Standing there in a full flowing skirt and a soft pink sweater with a lace collar, she was as delicate and feminine as the subject of a Renoir painting. Her hair was dark ashen brown, and she wore it pulled back from the fine bones of her face except for a soft fringe of bangs that angled across her forehead. She watched him with huge eyes that were a deep, pure gray.

Before her wits could scatter too far, Katie reined in her composure. She gave him a polite smile. "No," she said a little breathlessly. "My name is Kathryn Quaid. My store—Primarily Paper—is across the street from your building."

"Lucky me." Nick grinned, hoping to elicit a warm response from her. It didn't quite happen. The very corners of her mouth quirked upward, and he caught the hint of a sparkle in her eyes as she glanced away almost shyly.

"My partner and I want to welcome you to Briarwood, Mr.—?" She offered him the bouquet.

"Leone. Nick Leone," he said, accepting the flowers. He set the vase on the ledge of the bay window and reached out a hand to his new neighbor. "I'm *very* pleased to meet you, Miss Quaid."

Katie bit the inside of her lip as she grasped his hand. It was warm and firm. A sensation of heat suffused her as his hand engulfed hers. He hadn't looked quite so large from across the street. No less than a foot taller than she was, he loomed over her. He was nearly as tall as her brother, Rylan.

I don't want to be attracted to him, she told herself, trying to be practical. She was perfectly content going out with Michael Severs, a civil engineer, on an occasional date. They were good friends. Michael was nice and undemanding, while simply looking at this man had her rattled.

"...what kind of store?" Nick's voice broke into her wandering train of thought.

"Wallpaper and custom draperies," she said, cursing herself up and down. She was certain her lack of composure wasn't showing outwardly to any degree; she had too many years of practice at projecting a controlled image. But inside she was off balance, and she didn't like it. With a strength of will that belied her size she calmly proceeded with the conversation. "My partner and I are interior-design consultants."

"No kidding? That's great," Nick said, deciding to seize the opportunity as he accepted the business card she had plucked out of her skirt pocket. He studied the thing as if it didn't look like Chinese doodling to him. The fine script of the company name was a blur without his reading glasses, but there was no way he was putting them on now. "You're exactly the person I need."

Katie refrained from saying he was more in need of an optometrist than a decorator. He was holding her card upside down.

"Please, Mr. Leone, don't feel as if you're under

any obligation to make use of our services simply because we brought you a bouquet." She began inching toward the door. "I'd better be getting back. Again, welcome to Briarwood—"

"Don't rush off," Nick insisted, blocking the open doorway with his body, his hands braced against the jamb. He had a feeling that if he let her get away now, he might not get another chance. She was the first person he'd met who actually wanted to end a conversation, and he had a hunch it had something to do with the warm stirring of attraction between them. She was trying to give the appearance of being as cool as marble on the outside, but he sensed an underlying tension, which more than intrigued him.

Katie found herself staring at his chest. It was even more magnificent up close. Her heart gave a traitorous *ker-thump* she was certain he had to have heard. She took a step back and glanced up at him. "Really, Mr. Leone, I should—"

"—have a seat, a cup of espresso, and talk a little business," he said, finishing the sentence for her. Without waiting for her to acquiesce he took her by the arm and led her to a card table by one of the tall windows on the south side of the room.

Katie sat on an old folding chair and waited for him to return from the back room. The last thing she needed was to become involved professionally with the man. He struck her as being dangerous—in a way that had nothing to do with espionage and everything to do with disrupting her well-organized life. She would have to shove the job off on Maggie. She didn't feel she could refuse his business out of hand—that would be unpardonably rude. She caught herself hoping he had avant-garde taste. Then she would have a legitimate reason to turn him down. She and Maggie specialized in historic preservation and renovations.

"I'm turning the place into a restaurant," Nick said as he returned with two demitasse cups. He put one cup down in front of Katie and took the seat kitty-corner from her, setting his own cup down so he could gesture with his hands. "A nice place. Nothing elegant but really nice. Good Italian food. I've been thinking along the lines of antique furnishings. What do you think?"

As a sinking feeling of inevitability tugged at her, Katie worked the corners of her mouth up into a polite smile. "That sounds lovely." She decided to forgo subtlety in the hopes of finding a quick fix to her dilemma. "What does your wife think?"

Nick laughed out loud. It was a rather obvious question from someone who was trying hard to appear disinterested in him. "I'm not married. I realize I have a lot of work to do in here before I get to the decorating, but it's never too soon to start planning, right?"

"Of course," she said, her gaze scanning the empty room, more to keep from staring at him than anything else.

The store had been a fancy dress shop in Briarwood's early days. Katie could have recited the history of the place as if she were a tour guide. She knew every building in town of any historical significance. This one was a three-story brick building of Federal design that dated to 1803. It had stood empty for nearly two years. To have a chance to decorate it made her mouth water. But to work on it would mean having to work with Nick Leone, and that was a bad idea.

She glanced at him as he sipped his espresso. The tiny china cup looked distinctly out of place in his large hand. He seemed more the stoneware-mug type, she thought. It also seemed a tad unusual for him to offer her espresso. Wouldn't most men have had a cooler of beer in the back that they could dig into when the hot, dirty business of cleaning got to them?

The question reminded Katie of what she had come for in the first place. She had to make an effort to find out something about Nick before she returned to the store, or Maggie would never give her a moment's peace.

"Have you run a restaurant before, Mr. Leone?"

"I've worked at my share. What do you suggest for a color scheme?" he asked. It was all he could do to pay any attention at all to the conversation, sensing an undercurrent of sexual tension between them while watching her sit there as prim and proper as any Southern belle he'd ever seen in the movies.

"I don't know. What's your favorite color?"

She was trying to avoid his eyes, he decided as he purposely waited for her to look at him. He drew his lower lip between his teeth, as was his habit when he was concentrating. "Mmm. Dark green. At least, I think it's dark green." He made a face. "I'm just a little bit color-blind. See why I need your help?"

Katie's heart skipped so hard she lost her breath. Nick Leone's face was devastatingly masculine— all hard planes and angles tinted by the blue shadow of his beard. His nose was bold, high-bridged, not quite straight. His jaw was solid and square. Every time she started to feel the tiniest bit comfortable with his very masculine good looks, he gave her a crooked grin or made a boyish face. Her world had flipped upside down when he'd bitten his lip.

She took a long, deep breath to steady herself, inhaling the musty, dusty smell of the building, the aroma of espresso, and the faint tinge of sweat and man. "Have you decided what structural changes you're going to make?"

"I want to stick to the original floor plan as much as possible, but the upstairs will have to be opened up more. The first and second floors will both be set up with tables. The third floor and attic will be my apartment. I found some great junk up in the attic. Some of it might work as decorations or something. Come have a look."

She started to protest, but he seemed sincerely

enthusiastic, and her own curiosity about the artifacts was overwhelming. Her need to know overruled the budding pain in her lower back that warned her against scaling three flights of stairs.

Nick talked nonstop on their way up, pointing out bad steps and the original fireplace he already had uncovered in the second-floor parlor. Katie found his zeal contagious. Her decorator's eye could easily picture the finished rooms—stylish yet understated. She felt a definite sense of disappointment when she reminded herself Maggie would be doing the job.

"Isn't this floor great?" Nick said as they climbed the final stair to the gloomy attic. Katie had to admire his imagination. She barely could see the pine planking for the layers of dust and grime. "I'm thinking of installing skylights on the north side, or maybe dormers. Course, the restaurant comes first. I'm thinking out loud here—don't mind me. Here's the stuff I mentioned."

She could understand now how the antiques had been overlooked all this time. The attic was crammed with boxes and trunks, piles of old magazines, and racks of old clothes. Most of the junk was worthless. Obviously no one had mustered the fortitude necessary to clean out the mess in search of any potential treasures. Until Nick Leone had, she thought, as he rooted through a pile looking for more.

She was beginning to form the impression that Nick was a whirlwind of activity. He'd been in the building a matter of hours but had done more for it than anyone had in years. Since she'd come in, his body had either been moving or poised to move. He never seemed completely still.

"Where are you from, Mr. Leone?" she asked as she examined a display case of men's shirt collars from the turn of the century.

"Jersey. Call me Nick. You been here long?"

"All my life. What made you choose Briarwood?"

"I drove through here once a year or so ago and fell in love with the place. I'd always wanted to start a restaurant in a small town, so when I got the money together, I called a real estate agent, and here I am."

He made it sound as if it were the most logical thing in the world. Keeping an eye out for mice, Katie raised the lid on an old hatbox, uncovering a wonderful black bowler. "Why would you come to a small town in Virginia to start an Italian restaurant?"

"How many other Italian restaurants have you got here?" he asked, lifting a gaudy gold-fringed drape off a pile of old button-hook shoes.

"Good point."

"If I started a restaurant back home, it would have to be similar to everybody else's Italian restaurant. I'd have people all over me—'Nicky, why aren't you using my aunt Marie's cacciatore recipe? Nicky, why don' you have red-checked tablecloths? Your mama's taste isn't good enough for you, or what?'" Katie laughed as he thickened his accent for the impersonations. "'Nicky, why don' you hire my nephew Joey? He's a little slow, but he's a good worker.'" He made a comic face and raised his hands to his throat, pretending to choke himself.

For a moment he stood back and watched Katie laugh at his antics. Lord, she was lovely, he thought. Her face positively lit up when she laughed. When her laughter faded away, he cleared his throat and went on with his explanation. "Here I can do things my own way."

"No red-checked tablecloths," she said with a

sweet smile, wondering if he was such a soft touch that he would have given in to all those ridiculous requests. He didn't look like anyone's patsy. Or anyone's secret agent, she added, mentally shaking her head at Maggie's wild imagination.

Nick combed his hair back with his fingers and shrugged. "So what do you think of all this garbage?"

Hands on her hips, Katie sighed as she looked over what he'd found so far. "Most of this is from Aldeen's. It was a men's shop in this building from 1865 to 1917. A haberdashery."

Nick smiled at the way she drawled the long word. He could get used to her smooth, sweet voice. It appealed to him, especially because it was lower pitched than anyone would have guessed by looking at her.

His smile was growing on her much too quickly, Katie tried to warn herself. That wouldn't do at all. It was one thing to like him. Feeling her stomach flutter at the sight of his mouth hitching up on one side was altogether something else.

"Is it any good?" he asked, moving toward her. He wondered what the very proper Miss Quaid would think if he kissed her.

"Oh, yes," she said, watching him advance in her direction. "This could all work very nicely to create a unique atmosphere. Of course," she added, picking up a top hat and blowing the dust off in his face, effectively making him back away, "it would have to be cleaned first."

As Nick coughed Katie turned and started for the steps, determined to end her little visit with Mr. Leone before she could become any more attracted to him. Nick caught her from behind, his hands closing on her shoulders. She tensed beneath his touch, her whole body exploding with an awareness she didn't welcome but couldn't deny. Looking over her shoulder at him, she arched a brow in warning.

"Let me go first," he said. "I don't trust these stairs. I wouldn't want you to fall."

Not sure whether she was relieved or annoyed at his reason for touching her, she watched him descend ahead of her. This was a no-win situation. Her back had begun to ache in earnest. If she had gone down ahead of him, he would have seen how awkwardly the pain forced her to negotiate the steps. Following behind she had no way of controlling the pace of their descent. Gritting her teeth she started down behind him, determined to keep up.

"Are you interested in the job?" Nick asked.

"I'll have to discuss it with my partner and see if we can work you into our schedule. Are you certain you want to hire us? You haven't seen any of our work."

"Are you any good?"

"Yes. We're very good," she said, pride in her work ringing in her voice. She and Maggie had a wall full of awards and commendations to back up the statement.

Nick liked her confidence. "I'll take your word for it."

Reaching the landing above the last flight of stairs, he turned to smile at her just as Katie stepped wrong. Blinding pain shot through her. Her right leg buckled, and she lurched forward—right into Nick's arms.

"Are you all right?"

"I'm fine," she said through clenched teeth, blinking back tears. She was furious with herself for her weakness, and she tried in vain to push away from the rock-solid wall of his chest. "I just twisted my ankle, that's all." It was half of the truth.

"Damn these steps! I'm fixing them right away." He swung Katie up in his arms, a little frightened at how light and fragile she seemed, and started down the last flight of steps.

"This really isn't necessary, Mr. Leone," she said, protesting the way she felt in his arms more than the free ride to the ground floor.

Nick ignored her. "Do you want me to drive you to the hospital?"

"I don't need to go to the hospital. I'm fine. I just stepped wrong, that's all."

"Do you want me to get you an ice pack? Some aspirin?"

"I want you to put me down."

They had reached the bottom of the stairs, but Nick made no move to set Katie on her own two feet. His gaze had fastened on her mouth. It was wide and expressive, and he wanted very much to kiss it. Suddenly his breathing seemed labored, even though he was in good enough shape to run up and down the stairs all day without losing his breath.

"Mr. Leone."

He glanced up at her eyes. They were the color of storm clouds and held just as much warning. Deciding not to push his luck he eased her down, noting with a frown that she backed away from him as soon as her feet hit the floor. He wouldn't have minded keeping his arms around her for a few more minutes.

"You're sure you're okay?"

"Yes," Katie said, composing herself as she straightened her clothes and tried to ignore the erratic thumping of her heart. "Thank you for your concern. I'll be going now. Good-bye."

She started for the door, willing herself to walk normally and quickly. In the doorway she met Peter Ramsey from the police department, and Lee Henry Bartell. Katie nodded to the men but didn't stop to make conversation.

"Katie," both men said, nodding back. Ramsey's gaze followed her a second longer before he moved inside the building to take a look around.

Nick stepped into the doorway and watched Katie cross the street, noticing for the first time that her hair was held in a thick braid, the end of which twitched just above her waist as she walked.

"Pretty to look at, if that's all you want to do," Lee Henry said in a conspiratorial tone. He kept one eye on Officer Ramsey, who was out of ear-shot.

"You saying she's spoken for, or what?" Nick asked.

Bartell ran a hand over his thin frizz of salt-and-pepper hair and chuckled. "Miss Quaid speaks for herself."

"What the hell does that mean?" When they had met two days ago, Nick had decided he didn't like Lee Henry. The guy was a little too eager to dig into other people's business.

"It means, friend, if you're looking for a decorator or an ice princess, Katie Quaid is the lady to see."

"What'd you find out?" Maggie asked before Katie was even through the front door.

"Nothing." Katie stalked past her and around the counter. Heaving a sigh she leaned back against the edge of her desk and tried to will her-self past the need for a pain pill. She rubbed her palms up and down her arms, trying to erase Nick's touch and the warm tingling it had evoked.

"Nothing?" The redhead propped her elbows on the counter and slid her square black sunglasses down her nose. "You were over there for an hour. Y'all must've found *something* to talk about."

"He's converting the building into an Italian restaurant," she said. If she concentrated on the business aspect of her meeting with Nick, then she could avoid mentioning the other things she'd found out—such as how gorgeous he was up close and how his crooked grin could affect her cardiopulmonary system. "He wants to hire us as design consultants."

"Great!"

"Yeah. Have fun doing it," she said with no enthusiasm. The throbbing in her back echoed in her temples.

Maggie skipped over the remark. "What'd you find out about him? What about that gunshot wound?"

"I don't know, Mary Margaret!" Katie answered sharply. "What was I supposed to say to him? 'Nice to meet you, Mr. Leone. Hey, how'd you get that gaping wound in your shoulder?' "

Maggie pulled her sunglasses off, her brown eyes round with excitement. "It's a gaping wound in his shoulder?"

"I made that up!" Flames of pain seared her back and hip and burned down her right leg. Giving in, she reached for her purse and dug through it for her prescription bottle. "He didn't take his shirt off for me!"

"Too bad," Maggie said on a sigh. She watched as her friend popped open a plastic bottle and extracted a pill. Immediately she dropped her playful teasing. "Are you okay?"

Katie washed the medication down with flat diet cola and gave Maggie a weary wry smile. "Too many flights of stairs today. Mrs. Pruitt had me up and down from that guest room so many times, I felt like a human yo-yo. I've got to tell you, Maggie, that woman is going to drive me right over the edge. Mustard is the color for the room. Why won't she listen to me?"

Maggie smiled sympathetically. "It's all in how you tell her, darlin'. You have to talk her around until she thinks it was her idea."

"I know." Katie groaned in frustration. She realized Mrs. Pruitt was a perfect example of why she and Maggie had the ideal partnership. Katie's taste was impeccable, and no one could question her knowledge of period furnishing and decorating, but she was stubborn and opinionated. Maggie's lighthearted personality could charm the most contrary customer. She was a magician when it came to dealing with difficult people.

Katie's gaze scanned the empty room. "Zoe went home?"

"Yep. She wanted to stick around to find out more about Tall, Dark, and Greek God Bod, but she had to pick up Reese from Cub Scouts."

Katie rubbed her hands over her face, erasing the last remnants of her makeup. She pulled her braid over her shoulder and played with the end of it. "It's Reese's birthday Friday. Have you bought a present?"

"Uh-huh."

"Can I go in on it with you?" she asked tiredly.

"Your name's already on the card, sugar."

Katie wondered how long it would be before the emotional pain lessened enough for her to walk into a toy store. It had been five years since her accident, and still the results of it tore her apart inside. No one would have said so, but she knew Maggie could see it, because Maggie knew the whole truth of what her riding accident had done to her.

Maybe by the time all their friends had finished having children, Katie thought, maybe then she could be over the fact that she never could.

"You're a good friend, Mary Margaret," she said as the first welcome buzz of numbing medication sluiced through her.

"Yeah." Maggie slid her sunglasses back on. She went to lock the front door and turn the Open sign to Closed. "I'll even be a sport and drive you home. Let's blow this pop stand, Quaid."

TWO

SOMEHOW SHE KNEW it was him even before she looked up from the invoices on her desk. There was just something in the way the bells above the front door jingled that tipped her off. Katie looked up as Nick stepped around the counter. He had her china vase. In it white tissue paper skirted a tall stand of stiff green pasta.

"Good morning, Kathryn!" He smiled with all the brilliant warmth of the spring sun as he set the vase on her desk, then leaned back against the counter and crossed his ankles. He wore white socks and old brown loafers that looked as if they'd survived decades of fashion ups and downs.

Katie found herself eye level with a rather disturbing part of his anatomy. Men with bodies like this should be required to have a license to wear tight jeans, she mused, her cheeks flushing to a color that matched the flowers of her Laura Ashley dress. She straightened in her chair and forced her gaze up to his face. It was impossible not to return his smile.

"Good morning, Mr. Leone. What an unusual gift." She reached out a tentative finger to touch the sticks of pasta, not entirely sure what they were.

"Spinach fettuccine," he said. "I made it last night. Serve it with a little lemon butter." He kissed the tips of his fingers, then wagged one at her. "Eleven minutes. Don't overcook it. You'll ruin the texture."

"Thank you." She nodded and scanned her suddenly empty brain for something more to say. The only thing her brain could register was that she was relieved he was wearing a loose-fitting shirt. Unfortunately for her blood pressure, he had rolled the sleeves neatly to his elbows, calling attention to muscular forearms generously adorned with curling ebony hair.

"I fixed those steps Wednesday after you left. How's the ankle?" he asked, slipping his fingers into the pockets of his jeans, further straining the faded denim.

Katie swallowed hard and fixed her gaze on his left shoulder. "It's fine."

"You want me to look at it? I don't know anything about first aid, but I'd love to get my hands on your ankle," he said with a playful note in his voice.

Katie forced herself not to smile. "That's quite unnecessary," she said.

Nick grimaced inwardly. Even if she wasn't showing it now, he knew the lady had a sense of humor. Her face had glowed with it the other day. He wasn't about to believe that baloney he'd heard about her being the town ice princess. At any rate, he intended to do a little personal research into the rumor. "I got that stuff in the attic sorted out. I thought you might be able to tell me who could clean it."

"Certainly." She jotted down an address for him on a sheet of pink memo paper. Restoration was a much safer topic than Nick's hands on her ankle. The mere suggestion had given her a hot flash. "The people at the historical society in Charlottesville do a very nice job."

"I don't know where that is or what to tell them when I get there," he said, letting his fingertips brush hers as he leaned forward to take the scrap of paper. He thought he heard her breath catch in her throat. "Maybe you'd go along with me?"

"I'm sorry." Katie locked her gaze on her invoices. The look Nick was giving her was more hopeful than a spaniel puppy's. Calculated, no doubt, she thought, not holding it against him. No man could be as handsome as he was and remain totally unaware of his effect on women. "I'm very busy here, but I'd be glad to call ahead and talk to them for you."

The back screen door banged, heralding Maggie's arrival. She came in through the stock room, jabbering a mile a minute about why she was late. She was always late. The story about the knotted lace on her low black boots stilled on her tongue as she stepped into the office.

"Maggie!" Katie greeted her. Turning her back

to Nick, she gave her partner a meaningful stare. "This is Nick Leone. Mr. Leone, my partner, Maggie McSwain."

Maggie pulled her sunglasses off and gave Nick her best Southern-belle look, complete with batting lashes and sweetly pursed lips, her head tilted just so. She offered him her hand. When she spoke her voice was all magnolias and honey. "Why, Mr. Leone, it's such a pleasure. Katie just went on and on about meeting you the other day!"

Immediately Nick saw he had an ally in this little charmer with the hourglass figure. He was a man who read people very quickly and very accurately. He caught the mischievous gleam in Maggie's eyes—and the dire look in Katie's. "Really?" He smiled. "I was hoping Miss Quaid might accompany me to the historical society in Charlottesville today, but I guess she's too busy."

"Oh, pooh!" Maggie waved off the notion. "Don't be silly, Kathryn. Didn't you want to take those quilts of Emma Sweet's down there anyway?"

Katie ground her teeth and spoke through them all at once. "Mary Margaret, *darlin'*, I just was explaining to Nick, I'm much too busy, what with having to spend the day helping Mrs. Pruitt."

"*I'm* working with Mrs. Pruitt, sugar," she said, pressing a hand to her substantial bosom. She beamed a smile at Nick. "It must have slipped her mind."

Nick Leone was a dangerous man to be in a car with, Katie decided. It had nothing to do with his overwhelming masculinity or his boyish smile and everything to do with the fact that he drove like a maniac. The drive from Briarwood south to Charlottesville was lovely, the road winding up and down hills through sun-dappled woods. Nick attacked it with all the enthusiasm of a grand-prix driver.

"You wouldn't be practicing to try out for one of those car commercials, would you?" Katie asked dryly, grasping the armrest as the wine-colored Trans Am sailed through yet another S-curve. "You know, the ones that have little disclaimers down on the bottom of the screen. Do not attempt this with your own vehicle."

Nick winced, easing his foot off the gas. "I'm

so used to city traffic, when I get on a nice stretch of road, I tend to get carried away."

"You've lived in a city all your life?" she asked, deciding small talk was preferable to sitting there getting hot over the play of his thigh muscles beneath his jeans as he piloted the car.

He nodded. "Atlantic City and New York."

"I've been to New York," she said, remembering her trips to the National Horse Show at Madison Square Garden.

"Did you like it?"

She gave him an apologetic smile. " 'Fraid not. I guess I prefer small towns."

"Me too."

She studied him openly for a moment, deciding he meant those words even if they did sound funny coming from a former New Yorker. She also decided he had the most sincere eyes of anyone she knew. It was impossible for her to dislike him. The trouble was, she was going to like him too much. Why couldn't he have been arrogant, obnoxious, unscrupulous—something closer to Maggie's rumor of a ruthless spy?

"What did you do before you decided to go into the restaurant business?" she asked.

Nick glued his gaze to the road and repositioned his hands on the steering wheel. He didn't enjoy the idea of being evasive with her. "A little of this, a little of that."

"I didn't mean to pry," Katie said. "You're probably tired of people asking. I guess Southerners are just naturally nosey. If we were in New York, you'd probably tell me it's none of my business. And it's not," she added hastily. Turning to look out the window she rolled her eyes and cursed her sudden lack of tact.

Nick took pity on her and himself and decided to give her at least a portion of the truth. "I've been a waiter, a chef, a busboy, a cabdriver—all while I was trying to become a star on Broadway."

"You're an actor?" She was genuinely surprised because she'd never met an actor.

Nick grimaced. "That's a matter of opinion. I am a dancer—formal schooling, the whole bit."

"How wonderful!" And how envious she was. Since her accident, dancing was something she could only dream about. "Why wouldn't you want to tell anyone?"

He shifted his big body in the low car seat and shrugged uncomfortably. " 'Cause I didn't make

it, and I don't want to make a big deal out of it."
And because the kind of dancing he'd been do-
ing over the past two years was done *way* off
Broadway, he added mentally.

They took care of their business in Charlottesville quickly and lunched on deli sandwiches in a
park. Nick recited all the guidebook facts he'd
learned about the town and told Katie he was
going to come back one day to tour Thomas
Jefferson's home, Monticello. She told him about
her brother attending college there, at the Uni-
versity of Virginia, until their father's death had
forced him to return home to run the family farm.

On the drive back Katie marveled at how she'd
loosened up with Nick. He was so easy to talk to,
it seemed she'd forgotten that she didn't want to
get to know him—was afraid to get to know him,
she amended. Five years previously she had realized there could never be a Nick Leone in her life,
a man who made her feel warm inside, as though
he had let the sun in to fill all the dark, empty
places. She had resigned herself to the fact that
she could never have such a man because she
could never be the kind of woman he deserved.

Yet here he was, close enough for her to reach out and touch.

"Have dinner with me tonight," he said as they pulled up in front of Primarily Paper.

"Oh—Nick—" she stammered while her heart hammered in her chest. She shook her head. "I really should—"

"—say yes and go out with me." He grinned engagingly, his face much too close as he reached in front of her to open her door.

Katie scowled at him. "You have the most annoying habit of finishing my sentences for me."

"I'll pick you up at seven," he said, giving her braid a playful tug.

She stepped into the store just as a customer was leaving. Her polite professional smile for the woman quickly melted into a look that was almost comically distressed.

"I like him," Katie said woefully.

"Oh, no," her partner whispered dramatically, leaning over the counter. "We'd all better dress in black."

"It's not funny, Mary Margaret."

Maggie sighed and came around the counter to lead her friend to a chair at the oak trestle table.

Sitting down across from Katie she said, "What's so terrible about liking Nick Leone—except of course that he's a retired mercenary just back from the jungles of Central America?"

"Where'd you hear that one?" Katie asked, laughing.

"Stella Watkins, the food-sample lady at the supermarket," Maggie said with a chuckle, her eyes twinkling merrily.

Katie sobered. "He asked me to dinner."

"A fate worse than death. I'm sure I don't know how you'll be able to stand sitting across from that handsome man, gazing into those gorgeous brown eyes of his for a whole evening."

"Mag-gie!"

"Ka-tie! He asked you to dinner, not to have his baby. There's no reason you shouldn't go and enjoy yourself. Actually, it's your duty to go with him. You were duly elected to find out all about him. What's the problem anyway? You like Michael Severs. You go out to dinner with him."

"That's not the same," Katie argued. "Michael is safe. There's no danger of him becoming anything more than a friend, and he and I both know it."

"No fireworks."

"I don't want fireworks."

Maggie shook her head, her redheaded temper heating her cheeks. "You think you can't have fireworks. That's a lot of hogwash, Katie. You go out with Nick Leone and have a nice time with him and stop worrying about things that might never matter."

... Things that might never matter. Katie stood in front of the cheval glass in her bedroom and wondered bleakly how it could *not* matter. She was attracted to Nick. He was attracted to her. How could it not matter that the lower half of her body resembled a railroad map? Scars criss-crossed her abdomen in ugly silvery-pink lines—a thick, jagged one angled across her right thigh. Her knee wore a scalpel's crescent on each side. Her lower back bore similar marks.

No man had ever seen those scars. She was certain no man would ever want to. If she allowed her attraction to Nick to grow, and things took their natural course, what was she supposed to say to him when he first stared at this macabre artwork? By the way, Nick, I'm missing a few parts?

As she had lain in a hospital bed recovering, Katie had methodically replanned her life. There would be no career in show jumping because, after seventeen years of training, she could never ride again. There would be no husband because no man was going to find her desirable. There would be no children of her own. She would rebuild her life around her friends and her career as a decorator.

So far her plan had unfolded rather well. Oh, she knew there were men in town who called her an ice princess because she didn't let them get too close. And she knew she sometimes appeared aloof because she didn't cuddle and coo over other people's children. But she was dealing with her limitations as best she could, playing the hand she'd been dealt, as her brother Ry was fond of saying. She was respected in her field, proud of the business she and Maggie had built. She loved her work, had a busy life and a circle of good, close friends.

That had been enough—until she'd met Nick Leone.

She forced herself to concentrate on getting dressed. The camisole and tap pants she slid on were a silky rose pink. Her mauve linen skirt was gathered delicately at the waist. The spring-weight cotton sweater she pulled over her head repeated the shades of pink and mauve. Like everything that surrounded her Katie's clothing was feminine.

As she eased a comb through her waist-length dark hair, she studied the reflection of her surroundings in the mirror. Her house was a four-room cottage. Shades of peach ran throughout, accented with cream and touches of green. Everything in her home had been very carefully chosen, from the dainty white wicker headboard of her bed to her collection of heart-shaped porcelain boxes. Katie surrounded herself with feminine things to try to fill the hole her hysterectomy had torn in her own sense of femininity. Most of the time, it helped.

A thundering bark sent her to her front door. Nick stood at the gate of her small yard, wearing stylishly pleated khaki trousers and a white shirt with a band collar. He cradled a long loaf of bread in one arm and with wary brown eyes regarded Katie's Irish wolfhound.

"What's wrong, Nick?" she asked, coming forward to take hold of the enormous dog's collar. "Don't they have dogs in New Jersey?"

"Dog? That's a dog?" he questioned. "I swear I lost a bundle at Aqueduct on a horse that looked just like that."

Katie laughed, scratching the dog's head. "He's just an overgrown puppy."

"He's bigger than you are," Nick pointed out, coming through the gate of the picket fence. The happily panting wolfhound slurped his tongue along Nick's arm as he fondled the animal's ears. The dog's shoulder was at Katie's waist, and he looked as though he weighed a hundred and twenty pounds. Nick was certain Katie didn't weigh a hundred pounds dripping wet.

It pleased her how comfortable he seemed with her pet now. A farm girl at heart, Katie still measured a person's character by how they behaved around animals. She never quite trusted anyone who didn't like her dog. "His name's Watch. My brother gave him to me to keep an eye on me when I moved to town."

"I'll bet he serves his purpose." Nick formed a clear mental picture of an overprotective big brother sending this behemoth to keep scoundrels away from his baby sister. To the dog he said, "I'll bring you a bone next time, pal. The bread you've got your eye on is for the lady."

"First a bouquet of pasta, now a loaf of bread. You romantic devil," Katie teased, surprised at how lighthearted she felt now that Nick was there. He was a nice man, fun to be with. Maggie was right, there was no point worrying about complications at this point in their relationship. "You really are a chef at heart, Nick."

"Tonight I'm a chef who's tired of his own cooking. Let's go sample the local fare, Miss Quaid."

Nick was amazed at how little attention he paid to his dish of crabmeat and salty Virginia ham. There weren't many things that could distract his senses from a good meal. Katie Quaid did, though, with the way she tilted her head when she talked, the subtle quicksilver changes in her large gray eyes, her very proper posture and manners, the way she smiled and greeted friends who passed their table.

Her general manner was confident and straightforward, and Nick was sure that was how most people thought of her. Yet he sometimes sensed a hesitancy in her, as if she were afraid of someone finding a hole in her armor. As much a connoisseur of people as he was of fine food, Nick would have bet his last dime—if he hadn't already sunk it into his restaurant—that there was a lot more to Katie than met the eye.

They talked about their respective school backgrounds, Katie's college days at William and Mary, and how she had spent her spare time working in the restored colonial capital of Williamsburg. Nick told her about learning to cook from his mother and aunts and uncles. They touched on all the safe first-date topics.

"What's it like to be an interior designer?" he asked, cutting his fork through a piece of chocolate pecan pie. "Do you enjoy it?"

"Most of the time I love it," Katie answered, eyeing his dessert longingly. "The retail outlet for wallpaper and draperies keeps us busy, and as consultants we spend a lot of time going through houses with our clients to get an understanding of what they want done.

"I'm afraid I don't always have the required patience. Once in a while the people can be hard to work with—the lady who's determined to keep a moth-eaten moose head and funeral-parlor drapes in her new den, that kind of thing."

"I have a feeling your partner would be good at dealing with tough customers. Aren't you having any of this pie? It's delicious," he said, dipping his fork into the chocolate-sprinkled whipped cream that topped the triangle of scrumptious calorie-laden pie.

"I can't," Katie said on a sigh. Dessert was a rare treat because she couldn't work it off in rigorous exercise as she once would have.

Nick's eyes twinkled. He forked up another piece of pie and leaned across the small table to offer it to Katie. "One bite," he murmured seductively, easing the fork toward her mouth. "I promise it won't ruin that adorable little figure."

Temptation wasn't to be resisted when it was so mouthwateringly near. She took the treat into her mouth as Nick's dark gaze held hers. Suddenly, eating off her date's fork seemed as if it were the most intimate thing she'd ever done. She almost groaned at the heady sensation and at the rich flavor of the pie, then blushed when she realized several other diners were watching them.

Nick chuckled, but his expression suddenly went stony as the wailing of an alarm followed by sirens sounded in front of the restaurant.

Katie stared at him as he bolted from his chair, tossed some money on the table to cover the check, and dashed out the door. Out the front window she could see a group of teenage boys and older men milling around Nick's Trans Am with their hands to their ears and stunned expressions on their faces. A police car pulled up, and Peter Ramsey got out looking grim and official. Katie cautiously made her way outside, as confused as everyone else.

"I didn't mean to touch it!" one boy yelled above the din.

"It's okay, really!" Nick shouted as he fished for his keys and looked embarrassed. "It's just the alarm. I've been meaning to get it disconnected."

"Fella's got an alarm on his car," one old-timer said to another. The expressions on their faces clearly said they'd never heard of such a thing.

"Where'd you say he was from?"

"New York." Each raised his brows as if that said it all.

"That's a mighty unholy racket," Officer Ramsey commented as Nick reached into the car and turned the alarm off.

"I'm really sorry," Nick said, blushing as he glanced askance at the crowd that had gathered on the street.

Katie came to stand beside Nick.

"Evening, Katie." Ramsey's blue eyes lingered on her a moment. His frown deepened as he gave Nick a hard look. "We haven't had a car theft in Briarwood in nearly twenty years. You might keep that in mind."

"I will." Nick nodded as the policeman walked away. He rubbed a hand over his face and peeked through his fingers at Katie. Her fist pressed to her lips, she was trying valiantly not to laugh. The crowd was wandering away. "I can't believe *I* feel like an idiot because someone set off my car alarm. That's why I had the thing installed!"

"Nick, this is a small town," Katie said as she did allow herself to laugh. She shook her head, going around to the passenger's side of the car.

Nick slid into the driver's seat and unlocked her door. She eased herself down to the low bucket seat. "Most everyone here leaves their keys in the ignition and the windows rolled down."

"Ha! If you did that in New York, your car would be gone before you could put change in the meter."

He didn't drive her straight home. Instead he cruised the streets, pointing out to Katie reasons why he had moved to Briarwood, as if he needed to reassure himself after the embarrassing incident. The spring-evening sky was still light. People were working in their yards, tending their budding flower gardens.

"I think this place is great. Smell those trees and flowers," he said, breathing deep the sweet scents of boxwood shrubs and flowering dogwood trees and a thousand other rich green scents. "Incredible. It's like living in a greenhouse. And look at how many old homes and buildings have been preserved. Everyone seems so proud of the history here. It's fantastic."

Nick was so enthusiastic about everything. Katie couldn't help but be touched by his exuberant love for his new home. It won him a little more of her heart, because she loved Briarwood too.

"The location of the town is perfect," he said. "It's just far enough away from D.C. to be a small town instead of a suburb. And five thousand people seemed a large enough population to support another restaurant. Especially since there's also a healthy tourist trade. The fact that the college is nearby is a plus too."

He turned the car into the parking lot at the edge of Donner Park, just outside the main gates of Briarwood College. With most of the students on spring break the area was deserted as the day faded into night.

Katie shifted uncomfortably as her back began to ache. She'd spent too much time in the low car for one day. "Would you like to see the statue of the unknown Confederate war dead? He looks just like Charlton Heston," she said, hoping they could get out and stretch for a minute.

"I don't think so," Nick said softly. He watched her eyes, silvery in the half-light, widen slightly at his refusal. He leaned toward her, his hand reaching out so he could thread his fingers through her dark chestnut hair. "What I really want to do is kiss you, Katie."

Immediately there was pressure against his hand as she tried to lean her head away from him. He held firm.

"I don't think so, Nick," she said in a clear, strong voice. From long practice she appeared outwardly calm and controlled. Inside was a different story. As near as he was, she imagined she could feel the magnetic pull of his body on hers. She could feel her control slipping, and all he had done was state his intention. If just hearing him say the words would make her feel this way, what would playing them out do to her? The possibilities were frightening to someone who had taken such great pains to avoid emotional entanglement.

"Why not? What are you afraid of, Katie?" he asked, hoping he was pushing the right button to crack her veneer of control.

She raised her chin a stubborn fraction of an inch. "Nothing."

"Then kiss me," he said, drawing her toward him. "I dare you."

Rats, Katie thought. How had he known the

one thing to say? She knew herself well enough to know she wouldn't back down, even if she didn't feel ready.

She took a deep breath, telling herself all she had to do was keep her wits about her. She could kiss him and remain impassive. She could kiss him without losing her head. Slowly she leaned toward him, eyes wide open, and settled her lips against his. Everything she had told herself went up in smoke.

Nick's dark gaze locked on hers and clearly told her he wasn't going to let her have the upper hand. Hot and sweet, his mouth took hers, expertly stealing what power she'd thought she held. As he pulled her closer she felt engulfed, not only by the man, but by a wave of passion and need she had long held at bay. Nick unleashed it, and it took them both under.

He was as stunned as she when he lifted his mouth from hers to catch his breath. His blood was racing in his veins at a speed that made him dizzy. This had to be what it felt like to free-fall out of an airplane, he thought. His voice was a hoarse rumble as he looked down at Katie and said shakily, "I dare you to do that again."

Katie was beyond the logic that would have told her to back him off with an icy stare. She felt as if she had stepped off the edge of sanity and was falling through a warm, soft cloud of pure sensation. She met Nick halfway, something inside her eager to feel the sweet, frightening rush of adrenaline and desire again. It pounded in her chest, in her head, in her ears—pounded and pounded.

"Aren't you two a little old for parking?" a sarcastic voice drawled through Nick's open window.

Nick and Katie bolted apart, their eyes riveting on the face of Peter Ramsey. Neither had heard his squad car pull up. Neither had heard him knock on the door of the Trans Am.

"Park closes at nine," he said, tapping a finger to his wristwatch.

Katie glared at him. "Peter Ramsey, if I hear one word about this around town tomorrow, you *won't* live to regret it."

"Thank you for a very...unusual...evening, Nick," she said with a touch of dry humor to go with her wry smile. In spite of her initial misgivings she had to admit she was glad she'd let Nick talk her into a date. As if she'd had a choice, she thought. Katie imagined he could have talked donkeys into flying, with his adorable smile.

Nick grinned down at her in the yellow light from the brass coach lantern that hung beside her front door. He braced a hand against the door frame and rested the other on his hip. "I have to admit I've never come so close to getting arrested on a date before."

Catching an odd note in his inflection, Katie asked cautiously, "And when you weren't on a date?"

His smile became secretive. He ran a finger down the short, straight slope of her nose. "Let's just say I know what the inside of a jail looks like."

She didn't press for information but suddenly found herself wondering how he had broken his nose—it wasn't quite straight. He had told her he'd been a dancer, but he hadn't said when. Now he was telling her he'd been in jail.

Nick could almost hear the wheels turning in her brain. He wondered if she realized she had cocked a brow at him in that Scarlett O'Hara way of hers, or was it such an ingrained habit, she did it automatically. He knew one thing for sure—he had her puzzled. But her puzzlement could work to his advantage, he decided. Katie could be as aloof as a cat; perhaps she could be as curious. They had made it through their first date. Maybe if they could make it through a few more, he would tell her the rest of the story.

"Good night, Katie," he said, stepping back, shoving his hands into the deep pockets of his khaki trousers. "I'd kiss you again, but I think I've had all the excitement I can take for one night."

With a wink he turned and left her standing on her front step wondering which rumor might be true. Who had she just spent the evening with?

THREE

"MAYBE HE'S LIKE Dr. Richard Kimble in *The Fugitive*," Maggie mused, tapping her pencil against her pursed lips. She stared up at the ceiling and sighed. "A good man unjustly accused and on his way to his death until Fate moved its huge hand and whacked his train off the tracks."

"Right," Katie said with a teasing smile as she put the finishing touches to her sketch. She regarded her idea for the dining room of Nick's restaurant with a critical eye as she spoke. "That's just what I'd do if I were running from the law. I'd open a high-profile business like a restaurant."

Maggie made a face at her. "I was just having fun imagining."

Katie considered telling her friend what she knew about Nick's background but held back. Nick hadn't wanted to tell anyone about his dancing days in New York. She would respect his wishes and let Maggie go on having fun speculating.

Finishing her coffee, Zoe stood up from the table and slung her tote bag over her shoulder. "Shirley Carson heard he used to be a security chief at a Pontiac plant in New York."

"That makes an even dozen theories," Katie said, adding more green shading to the drapes in her sketch.

"Is that including the one about him being the prodigal son of a wealthy industrialist?" Zoe asked, chuckling as she headed for the door.

"Thirteen," Katie corrected herself.

Zoe laughed. "See y'all later. I'm off to work."

"Bye, Zoe," Maggie and Katie said together as their friend left.

"And what's your theory, Kathryn?" Maggie asked, standing and smoothing a hand down the skirt of her emerald-green dress. "You've been out with him twice now."

Katie fixed her gaze on her sketch. She'd had her second date with Nick—they'd gone to an adventure movie at the town theater—and he was still a mystery to her. He was a man with a mysterious past and a mysterious ability to make her forget her deficiencies as a woman. He was a man who made her want to be with him and want to run away all at once. The moth to the flame theory, she thought to herself, but she didn't share her thoughts with Maggie. She wasn't ready to yet. "I think he's a very nice man who's come here to live a quiet life."

"Has he said anything about that gunshot wound?"

"No, and I'm not going to ask." Katie gathered up her portfolio and headed for the door. She was the last person who would grill someone about an injury. She could remember too well how she had hated having people ask for all the gory details about her accident once she had finally been able to come home.

In the open doorway of Nick's building she nearly ran head-on into a balding fat man with a bulbous nose and thick frowning forehead. He stood in Katie's way, staring at her as if he had no manners whatsoever. She could just see over the man's slouching shoulder. Nick stood a good ten feet behind him with a murderous scowl on his face.

"Pardon me," she said.

The fat man grunted and stepped out of her path, then left.

"Who was that?" Katie asked.

"The county engineer. Charming guy, don't you think?" Nick said sardonically. He ran a hand through his hair, dislodging little particles of plaster. There was a smudge of plaster dust on his square chin, and a thin layer of the stuff coated his black T-shirt. "He just told me I've got to cough up forty-five hundred bucks for a new curb and gutter before he'll issue my remodeling permit. And he seemed to take unusual pleasure in telling me."

Katie frowned in concern. "Can you manage it?"

He gave a harsh laugh. "Sure, but then I won't need the permit. That's half my remodeling budget."

He swore under his breath as the phone rang two flights above them. The phone company had yet to hook up a new phone on the ground floor. Now he had to wonder if he could afford it. He glanced distractedly at Katie. "You brought those sketches. Come on upstairs."

He turned and bolted up the steps two at a time, yelling to the phone that he would be right there.

Katie followed at her own pace, her heart heavy over Nick's problem. People could cross off all their wild theories that involved his having a lot of money. He was operating on a shoestring, doing much of the work himself, and had obviously sunk every nickel he had into his dream. Despite the warnings of her cautious heart, Katie had become very fond of Nick over the past two weeks. She hated to see something bad happen to him.

"...yeah, Uncle Guido, I know. I know, but you gotta do it. You gotta get rid of him, he's a bum. Vinnie warned you the guy wasn't worth the space he took up. Lose him."

Katie's eyes widened as she stood on the third-floor landing clutching her portfolio in front of her.

"I know it's tough, but it's business, you know. Yeah, yeah, yeah, I'm coming back for the trial. What'd you think—that I wouldn't show? No. Right. Say hello to everybody for me. Bye." With a sigh, Nick hung up the phone and looked around. "Katie?"

She peeked around the doorway. "I didn't want to intrude," she said in a small voice. Trial? she wondered.

He waved it off and went to the refrigerator. "My uncle Guido and his labor disputes. He's a bricklayer. He hired his sister-in-law's son-in-law as a favor. The guy's a deadbeat, but Guido doesn't have the heart to fire him. You want a soda or something?"

"No, thanks." She took a seat at the Formica-topped table and let her gaze wander. It wasn't hard to guess at Nick's priorities. The kitchen was immaculate. Little clay pots of growing herbs lined the window ledge above the sink. There was a rope of fresh garlic hanging to one side of the window. Cookbooks and gourmet gadgets lined the counter. Across the hall his bedroom was a jumble of bedsheets, shirts, jeans, and abandoned shoes.

Nick popped the top of his soda and slumped onto a chair. What a lousy day, he thought, and it wasn't even noon yet. His uncle, the county engineer, then there'd been that little bit of information he'd picked up after running into Peter Ramsey at the gas station. He leveled his dark gaze at Katie. "Why didn't you tell me you were involved with that cop?"

"Peter Ramsey?" she asked, incredulous. "I'm not involved with him."

"But you were," Nick said, pressing the issue. He sat up and leaned his elbows on the table. "I heard you were practically engaged!"

"Oh!" Katie nearly choked on a mixture of surprise and anger. "We were not! I went out with him a few times. Things didn't progress the way he wanted, and that was the end of it."

"I just wish you would have told me." He pouted, scratching his arm. He knew he was only making the day worse by acting like an idiot. It was none of his business who Katie had dated in the past. It only concerned him because he was quickly developing a wide possessive streak when it came to her. Some irrational part of him wanted to think he was the only man she'd ever been interested in. "I'm trying to make a good start in this town. I don't want to antagonize the police department by trespassing on their territory."

Katie jumped out of her chair, needing to be taller than Nick for once. She glowered down at him, her hands perched on her slender hips. "I am not Peter Ramsey's territory! I am not *anybody's* territory. This is Virginia, not the wild West." She stepped back and shook her head. "You are absolutely amazing. Half the town thinks you're a cross between Al Capone and James Bond, and you're worried about something so stupid!"

"They think *what*?" Nick asked, his dark brows shooting up in surprise.

Katie planted her hands on top of her head and rolled her eyes. "Me and my big mouth. I'm sorry, Nick, but this is a small town—gossip is the number one pastime. You haven't been very forthcoming about your background, so, naturally, rumors have run rampant."

"They think *what*?"

"Well . . . there are lots of theories."

Nick watched her shifting uncomfortably from

foot to foot. It was amusing to see Katie Quaid squirm. She wasn't a lady who lost her composure easily. "Such as?" he questioned.

"Oh...they range from you being a former agent for the CIA to being a retired international art thief to being a protected witness to being a ruthless mercenary."

He broke up, laughing so hard he got a stitch in his side. "Me? Ruthless? A mercenary? A spy? Me?"

"Those are some of the more popular rumors." She frowned at him. "That doesn't make you angry? I thought you'd be furious."

"It's too funny! I'm the last guy—I mean, I may have a checkered past, but I was an Eagle Scout, for crying out loud!"

"Then what was that you said to your uncle about going back for a trial?" she demanded, letting slip the fact that she'd been eavesdropping on his conversation.

Nick sat back in his chair, trying to catch his breath. He rubbed his side and took a long swallow of his cola. "A couple of weeks before I moved down here I happened to be in a store when some goofballs tried to rob the place. I got shot, actually the bullet only grazed my shoulder. I have to go back to testify at the trial."

Katie was torn between relief and sick fear. The thought of Nick getting shot in a holdup made her throat constrict. She sat back down and brushed her bangs out of her eyes. "And what about your statement about knowing what the inside of a jail looks like?"

"A simple misunderstanding," he said, giving her his most innocent look. He wasn't quite ready to tell her he'd been the entertainment for a "ladies only" night at a club and the place had been raided. Poor Katie, he thought, suppressing a chuckle, she'd had enough revelation for one day. She'd struck up one of her Southern-belle poses but looked annoyed and embarrassed instead of cool and serene. "Don't tell me you believed those rumors."

She gave him a look. "I know better than to believe ninety-nine percent of the rumors that fly around a small town. Do you think I would have gone out with you if I believed you were some sort of thug?"

"I dunno." He shrugged, playful lights dancing in his dark eyes. He leaned across the table to run his finger down her nose. "Maybe you're one of those ladies who gets excited by that kind of thing." Her icy glare made him laugh again. "You know, maybe these rumors will actually be good for business. I could center an ad campaign around them. 'Eat at Nick's—it's an offer you can't refuse,'" he said in a rough voice.

Katie rolled her eyes, trying not to grin. She was relieved he was taking the rumors so well. The townspeople didn't mean any harm. They were just curious. Deciding it was time to lay the topic to rest, she asked, "Do you want to see my sketches now?"

"Yeah, sure," he said, standing up and ambling toward the bedroom, fluffing white powder out of his hair. "But let me change my shirt first. This plaster dust is making me itch."

She told herself she wouldn't look, promised herself she wouldn't look. She looked. She exhaled so hard, her lungs hurt. Nick's back was a lesson in classical art. Smooth, dark skin was stretched taut over an array of muscles that rippled beneath the beautiful surface.

He dropped the black T-shirt carelessly on the floor beside the bed and looked over several possible replacements hanging on various parts of the open door. He settled on a red T-shirt that had been snagged over the doorknob.

"So, did you come up with any good ideas?" he asked, strolling back into the kitchen with the shirt dangling from his fingertips, ostensibly unconcerned that he was only half dressed.

A wave of heat washed over Katie. Her heart spun like a top. He belonged on a poster. A hunk poster. A super-hunk poster. His black hair spilled onto his forehead. A sweetly boyish grin kicked up the corner of his mouth. His chest was no disappointment. Sculpted muscle was thickly forested with ebony curls. The curls arrowed down around his slightly off-center navel and disappeared into the waistband of his jeans. Just to the right of his belly button he had the cutest little mole shaped like a crouching bunny. And unless she was looking for it, she'd never have noticed the tiny pink scar on his shoulder. Gaping wound, indeed, she thought with a laugh.

"Ideas?" she asked blankly. Boy, did she have ideas! She was having ideas she hadn't had in years.

Eyes twinkling, Nick pulled his shirt on over

his head. The name of a trendy Washington nightclub was emblazoned across the front. He watched Katie's gaze follow the descent of the bright red fabric down his chest and over his belly. He thought she was going to faint when he tucked the bottom into his jeans. "Ideas for the dining room. Remember the dining room?"

Realizing she'd been staring, Katie blushed and fumbled with her portfolio. What was the matter with her, losing her wits and her manners over an attractive arrangement of muscle and bone. "Yes. I think I've come up with several good ideas, all of them fairly simple, all with a Victorian feel to them to tie in with the things you found in the attic."

She pulled out the rough sketches she'd made and handed them to Nick. He leaned back and squinted a little. When he couldn't extend his arm any farther or lean back any more, Katie reached across the table and pulled the drawings toward her.

"Is this better?" she asked dryly. "Or should I go across the hall?"

Nick scowled. He reached into a drawer beside him and pulled out a pair of round, wire-rimmed reading glasses. The look he gave Katie was half warning, half pleading. "Don't tease me."

He was self-conscious about such a little thing as wearing reading glasses? Katie's hand automatically went to her belly, smoothing over the soft cotton of her skirt and the scars that lay beneath it.

"This is too frilly," Nick said, setting aside one sketch. He pulled his lower lip between his teeth as he considered the other two. "I like this one best." He held out the sketch that pictured the finished room furnished with small Victorian side chairs tucked under small square tables draped in green and tan. The walls were adorned with the hats, walking sticks, shirt collars, and other things he had discovered in the attic.

"Is that the color you had in mind?" she asked, pointing her pencil at the hunter-green drapes she'd drawn at the tall windows.

"Is it dark green?" he asked with a crooked smile.

Katie nodded, biting her lip. Sometimes he was just too cute to be resisted.

He grinned. "Then that's it."

"Maybe this is a silly question, but if you can't

tell whether or not it's dark green, how do you know dark green is your favorite color?"

Nick just shrugged and went on grinning. He took wicked pleasure in seeing Katie off balance. It was such a contrast to her usual state. She didn't enjoy it any more than a cat enjoyed a bath though. She was laughing at him, but he could see she was annoyed with herself for slipping off her pedestal of composure. Silver flashed in her eyes like lightning in storm clouds.

Shaking her head Katie took the drawing and jotted some notes on it, then tucked them all into her portfolio. "I can start keeping an eye out for furniture. We'll need six to eight weeks on the drapes, so let me know when you're ready to look at fabric. They'll be one of the bigger expenses. You might want to consider going without them on the second floor for a while. The woodwork up there isn't bad."

He nodded. "With this curb and gutter surprise, I may have to hold off working on the second floor anyway. I think I can get twenty tables in the main-floor dining room. That wouldn't be a bad start."

"I'm sorry this had to happen, Nick. Unfor-

tunately for you a change of ownership sometimes stirs up unknown problems. This building
had been vacant for a long time."

"It's just the breaks of business." He reached
across the table and squeezed her hand. "Thanks
for caring, Katie. It helps to have good friends."

His voice seemed as warm as the hand that held
hers, yet shivers chased over Katie's skin, raising
goose bumps. She liked it when Nick touched her.
She liked it too much.

Clearing her throat nervously she slipped her
hand from his and stood up. Nick rose as well.

"I'd better be getting back to the store. Maggie
has a consultation at eleven."

"Katie," he said softly, catching her hand as she
turned for the door. His heart thudded as she
looked at him. There was a split second of astonishment in her eyes, as if she were surprised he
wanted to touch her. The lady didn't know how
much he wanted to touch her, Nick thought, gritting his teeth against a surge of desire. Sometimes
she looked so vulnerable, so in contrast to the
Katie she usually presented to the world that he
wanted to hold her and protect her and make love
to her. "I'm sorry about earlier. I was obnoxious.

This morning didn't get off to a great start, and when I heard that rumor about you and Ramsey... I guess I got jealous."

"Jealous?" Katie asked with wonder. This gorgeous man was jealous because she had once dated a mere mortal?

"Yeah," he murmured, easing his arms around her. "Jealous. That surprises you?"

"Sort of," she whispered, almost unable to hear her own voice for the pounding of her heart. She met his lips when he dipped his head down to steal a kiss. "Nick?"

"Hmm?" he stole a second kiss and breathed in the soft scent of honeysuckle that clung to her dark hair.

"I like your glasses."

His smile was tender and endearingly appreciative. "Thanks."

He kissed her again, slowly, deeply, his tongue searching out hers for gentle play. There was no ice in this princess, he thought as he drank in her sweet warmth. Behind the cool and competent lady was a woman with needs and secrets in her eyes, a woman he wanted more than he had a right to.

Katie clung to him, using his wide shoulders as an anchor in the storm of desire that flared between them and threatened to overwhelm her. How could it be so strong, so tempting? she wondered. It was unlike anything she had ever known, and she wasn't sure how to deal with it.

"Katie," he whispered, dragging his mouth along her jaw to her ear. His hand slipped under her sweater and found her small round breast. He cupped it, kneaded it.

"Nick, I have to go," she said, backing away from him, a faint note of panic in her voice. She needed time to think, something she obviously couldn't do in Nick's arms. She bent to pick up her portfolio, wondering when she had dropped it. Her hair spilled over her shoulder. She threw it back with a hand that wasn't quite steady. "I have to go."

"Katie, wait," he said, following her down the steps. He wasn't at all sure he knew what had just happened, but it didn't take a genius to see Katie didn't want to discuss it.

Katie forced herself to stop on the landing before the last flight of stairs. She was acting like a crazy person because his kiss had made her feel as if she were going to go up in flames. She turned to face Nick, trying hard not to look the least bit confused.

Nick stopped on the step above her, bracing his hands against the wall on either side. "Are you free Saturday night? I thought we could go dancing. There's this club in D.C.—"

"No, I can't, Nick. I'm sorry," she said, disappointment forming a knot in her throat. "I don't dance."

He teased her with a smile. "Everybody can dance. All you need is a fabulous instructor like myself."

She glanced away from his eyes, forcing the corners of her mouth up in a phony grin. "That's probably true, but I'm tied up on Saturday."

"Oh." He stepped down to her level and wound a finger into her long hair. "Are you mad at me?"

Katie looked up. His eyes were so brown and so sincere. He was so sweet, it made her heart ache. "Why would I be mad at you?"

His broad shoulders lifted in a shrug as he dismissed the notion. He bent his head and pressed a kiss to her lips. "You're so pretty," he murmured against her mouth.

A magnetic pull was urging her toward him again. Before it could overrule her good judgment, Katie put a half step of distance between them. "There's a concert Sunday in the park. We have a pretty good chamber orchestra...if you like that kind of thing."

"I do." He smiled, relaxing. "It's a date."

Maggie was ready to go out the back door as Katie came in the front, which suited Katie fine. She needed a little time to herself. She hung the Gone to Lunch sign on the front door, took the phone off the hook, and went to sit on a box in the stock room where she could stare out the screen door at the beautiful spring morning.

Decision time, Katie, she told herself. The kind of desire she'd felt in Nick's arms didn't come along every day. In fact, she'd never experienced it before. But what was she supposed to do about it? Did she do the safe thing and break it off with Nick now, or did she let him become the first man to get close to her since her accident? She knew what her heart wanted, but her heart wanted a lot of things it could never have.

Nick seemed so special. Everything clicked when they were together. Just like in the movies—she heard bells, she saw fireworks. Those were things she had always been too practical to believe in before. She wanted to go on seeing him. She wanted more. She wanted to go dancing with him. She wanted to be whole. Instead she was scarred and incomplete. He would have seen that, if she hadn't backed away from his lovemaking in the kitchen. He would have seen that the pretty package that attracted him was a battered, empty box under the feminine wrapping.

Lifting her heavy mane off her neck Katie sighed up into her bangs. Life had seemed a lot simpler before Nick Leone had come along with his mysterious past and velvet brown eyes. But she realized it would seem a lot lonelier without him.

Maybe it was time she took a chance. She'd been so careful for so long. She couldn't read Nick's mind. She couldn't know if he was interested in her on a long-term basis. She couldn't know if he would be able to overlook her scars, or if children were important to him. But she didn't have to read his mind to know he was a nice man. She didn't have to read his mind to know he wanted a deeper relationship. She wanted one too.

Maybe it was time to stray a little from the path she'd so carefully mapped out for herself five years ago. To pass up the chance would be the coward's way out, and if there was one thing Katie had tried hard not to be in her life, it was a coward.

Nick sat on the steps and let his gaze roam around what would one day be the main dining room of his restaurant. He needed to install new light fixtures. The floor had to be sanded and re-finished. He didn't even want to think what needed to be done to make the back room into a functional kitchen. Upstairs there were dropped ceilings to be removed, walls to be knocked out.

Forty-five hundred bucks. He groaned. He'd al-ready borrowed all he could. He would have to fork over the money for the curb and gutter now so he could get the permit, and then make the money back some way so he could afford to do the necessary remodeling.

There was one sure way he could make enough money in a relatively short amount of time. All he had to do was pick up the phone and say yes to Jack Clark's standing offer. They would have to haggle a little over scheduling, and Nick would have to negotiate for a percentage of the gate, but it was the best solution. It was the only solution.

"Looks as if I'll be doing some dancing after all, Katie," he said, wondering what proper Katie would have to say when he told her he was going to solve his financial problems by going back to his old job as the Highwayman—the hottest male erotic dancer on the East Coast.

FOUR

KATIE HAD COMMITTED her Saturday morning and afternoon to working on the town project. Saturday night was going to be devoted to recuperating from working on the town project. She decided the best thing she could do was work so hard, she would have little energy left over to devote to wondering if Nick had found someone else to go dancing with him.

The town project was known as the Drewes mansion. Myra Mason-Drewes had willed the estate to the city. It had been badly in need of repair and, even though Myra's wish had been that the estate be restored, the town council nearly had decided to tear it down. Katie and a group of other citizens concerned about historic preservation had talked them out of it.

Professionals had been called in for the nuts and bolts restoration work, but costs had been kept low by having townspeople devote their time and talents to the simpler tasks. By late summer the Drewes mansion would be added to the walking tour of Briarwood that included a number of other historic buildings. The tourism committee was planning a gala party to celebrate the opening and raise funds to help cover some of the costs.

The sounds of hammers pounding and power saws whining above the country music coming from a portable radio in the kitchen brought a smile to Katie's lips as she dipped her paintbrush into the bucket again. By the end of the day all the noise would probably give her a headache, but she wouldn't think about that now. She was going to enjoy the feeling of camaraderie that came from working beside people she had known all her life. It was one of the joys of living in a small community. She also thoroughly enjoyed the actual work of fixing up the house. Preserving a piece of the past was a labor of love, as far as Katie was concerned. She threw a happy smile at Maggie, working nearby on painting window trim.

"Katie, the walls in the dining room are ready to paint. Should we go on ahead and start?"

"Sure, John. Just make certain all the drop cloths are in place," she called back without taking her eyes off the window frame she was painting. The woodwork in the parlor had been stripped of nineteen coats of paint, including layers of hot pink and lime green. Her brush spread a layer of rich cream over the wood. Eventually all the rooms in the colonial home would be returned to their original color schemes.

"I hope y'all appreciate just how much I hate painting trim," Maggie said to no one in particular. She stuck her tongue between her teeth as she ran a narrow brush along the wood between two panes in the twelve-over-twelve-pane window. She glanced over her shoulder to the next wall where Katie was working. "However, I don't mind being the lookout. Guess who's coming up the front walk, Kathryn."

"Tom Selleck."

"Close, but no mustache. It's none other than the mysterious Mr. Leone, heartthrob of Fairfax Street."

Heartthrob. What an inadequate word, Katie thought. Beneath her baggy pink T-shirt her heart was throbbing all right, but that was the least of what Nick could do to her with nothing more than a glance.

She dropped her paintbrush and tried to straighten her hair, only succeeding in streaking ivory paint through the strands that had escaped her braid. Now that she had made a decision about an ongoing relationship with him, she felt skittish, as if Nick would somehow know by looking at her that she had decided to take the monumental step.

"Morning, Nick!" Maggie said, beaming a big smile at him as he came in. "What is that delicious aroma?"

"Hiya, Maggie." He grinned, lifting an enormous roasting pan. "I brought lunch. Lasagna. Are you people hungry or what?"

"Starved. Ravenous. Famished," Maggie answered. She abandoned her post to lift the lid on lunch. Nick chuckled at her heartfelt groan as she stared longingly at the dish he'd prepared.

"Nick, you didn't have to cook for all these people!" Katie exclaimed. There were easily a dozen people working in the house and several more outside.

"All these people? This would have been a slow day in my mother's kitchen."

"You're from a large family, Nick?" Maggie asked.

"Huge. You practically had to have reservations for a place at the table. It was great."

Katie ignored the little twinge of warning she felt. So he had enjoyed growing up in a large family. What did that have to do with the two of them? Nothing, she firmly told herself.

"John Harris said everyone was devoting their best talents to this job," Nick said, setting his roaster down on a table that was a sheet of plywood over two sawhorses. He lifted the lid off the pan. Immediately three people poked their heads into the room through various doors, their noses twitching. Nick gave what Katie thought was an adorable shrug and said, "Me, I can cook a little bit."

His was an understatement Katie realized a few minutes later after sampling his cooking. Nick's lasagna was far removed from what Katie was used to buying frozen. Everything in it was absolutely fresh and perfectly prepared. The tomato sauce was bursting with sweet flavor. The variety of herbs and spices were a delight to the taste buds. The cheese had that special bite that told Katie it was freshly grated. The combination of ingredients had resulted in a masterpiece.

"This is heaven," Katie said with a sigh. She and Nick sat side by side under a magnolia tree in the front yard, eating their lunch from paper plates. In addition to the lasagna he'd brought loaves of warm garlic bread. Everyone had chipped in for soda and beer, and Mavis Davies had provided two pans of her special chocolate-chip brownies for dessert. "I'm going to write to the people who package those diet dinners and tell them they've got a nerve calling the stuff they make lasagna," Katie said.

Nick frowned at her. "You buy frozen stuff? To eat?"

"I'm no cook. If it doesn't come with microwave instructions on the box, I can't make it."

He shuddered and muttered something in Italian that sounded like a prayer. His warm brown eyes found Katie's and he said earnestly, "Cooking should be a joy, just as eating should be a joy."

"Well," she said, scooping up another forkful of lasagna. "I can promise you, if I cook it, it won't be a joy to eat."

"Didn't your mother teach you to cook?"

"My mother left when I was ten," she said almost matter-of-factly. "My father cooked, my brother cooked. I was too busy with other things."

"I'm sorry," he said quietly. "I didn't know."

"Of course you didn't," she said as she attacked her dessert.

There was a finality in her tone that suggested the topic was closed. Nick wouldn't let go quite that easily. He wanted to know who Katie was. Bitting into his own rich square of chocolate dessert, he made a mental note to get the recipe from Mavis. "That must have been rough on you, growing up without a mother."

Katie's shoulders lifted in a stiff shrug. "She wasn't a very good mother. The thing I remember most about her was that she hated the farm and did everything she could to make her feelings known to everyone."

She didn't say anything about the feelings of confusion that had haunted her after her mother's desertion. She had vowed then that someday she would have children of her own, and she would be the best mother in the world. But she didn't mention it to Nick. She didn't tell him it was just one of her dreams as a young girl that had been shattered and left in pieces on a jump course in upstate New York.

"You should have told me about this project, Katie," he said, reproaching her gently to bring her thoughts back to the present. He hadn't enjoyed the haunted look that had crept into her pewter-colored eyes or the sensation that she had pulled away from him for a moment, drawn into herself.

"I thought you had your hands full working on your own place," she said. "I didn't want you to feel obligated to work here too."

"It's a community project. I want to be part of the community."

She could see how eager Nick was to be a part

of the small town, to get involved and make friends. He would have felt hurt if no one had asked him to join in. She reached up with her napkin to wipe a speck of chocolate off his chin. "I'm sorry. I guess I wasn't thinking."

"Yeah, well, just don't let it happen again." He gave her a warning look that had her giggling, then he grinned his endearingly crooked grin and winked at her.

Katie said, "You're here now, and we'll work you till you drop, but I can guarantee you a dozen devoted customers when you finally open the restaurant. This lunch was great. Thanks for bringing it."

"My pleasure. I'll do what I can to help this afternoon, but I have to knock off around four. I have to go to D.C. tonight."

Katie tried to look casual while she wondered if she'd missed the boat. "Oh? Got a hot date?"

"No," Nick said with a chuckle. She was so cute when she tried to act casual about something she was dying to know, like a cat trying to appear aloof when someone was trailing a string of yarn in front of it. "It's business. I'm gonna help out this friend a couple nights a week to make the money I need for my remodeling."

He set his plate aside and slipped his arm around Katie. She looked so young in her paint-spattered jeans and T-shirt, with no makeup and her hair mussed, he half expected her father to come out on the front step and chase him away. He leaned down and pressed a quick kiss on the tip of her nose, murmuring in a husky voice, "I'm not interested in going dancing with anyone but you, kitten."

If that was true, it was going to be a while before Nick got to go dancing again, Katie thought ruefully. She pushed her own disabilities from her mind to concentrate on getting to know Nick better. "You've been trained as a dancer, worked as a dancer, and you still want to go out dancing. You must really love it."

"I do. Dance is the ultimate combination of art and athleticism. It's beautiful, powerful, entertaining," he said, trying to concentrate on Katie instead of the butterflies in his stomach. This seemed like the ideal time to tell her. He was going to leave in a few hours to meet with Jack Clark to finalize the details of the return of the Highwayman. He took a deep breath and plunged in. "I love it. I've danced on Broadway, off Broadway, as a lead, in the chorus line, as a stripper."

Katie shot him an amused look and burst out laughing.

"Really," Nick said, trying to laugh along. "For two years."

"Uh-huh, right." Katie shook her head and pushed herself to her feet. Nick was self-conscious about putting his reading glasses on in front of people. Dancing around in his birthday suit was simply out of the question. A stripper. How absurd. One thing she really liked about Nick was his ability to make her laugh.

Mavis Davies stuck her head out the door of the house. "Katie, Richard is out back with that countertop. Are we ready for it?"

"Yes. I'll be right in, Mavis." She started for the house, then glanced back at Nick. "Are you ready to get to work, Gypsy Rose Leone?"

She clearly didn't believe him. Nick cast his gaze heavenward as Katie walked away. "I tried," he whispered, scolding himself inwardly for being too much of a coward to try harder. Katie was busy, he rationalized. This really wasn't the best time to tell her.

It wasn't that he was ashamed of being an erotic dancer. He was proud of putting together a tasteful, artistic, entertaining routine. He saw nothing objectionable about the performance he gave as the Highwayman. The problem was explaining it and making Katie understand. He didn't look at it as taking his clothes off for a living. Nick thought of it as providing fun, escapist entertainment, but knew there were a lot of people who wouldn't agree with his point of view. He had known his share of proper ladies who had considered him some sort of second-class citizen once they'd found out what he did for a living. He had to hope Katie wasn't one of them, he thought as he picked up their plates and followed her to the house.

Not only did Nick gain prospective customers by showing up, he gained friends as well. After what Katie had told him about the rumors going around, he was a little nervous at first that he might not be accepted, but everyone was friendly and glad to have an extra hand. While they enjoyed speculating about the new guy in town, they didn't seem to take the rumors seriously. The general mood was one of fun. And they were happy to be contributing to something that was for the good of the community.

There were at least ten other people working around the house. Nick learned one thing about all of them—they liked and respected Katie and clearly thought of her as their leader even though she was younger than most of them. He felt proud when he looked at the lady who had become so important to him in such a short amount of time.

With her hands on her hips Katie looked at the dining-room wall, which was much taller than she was, and said, "We need more ladders."

"I know," John Harris said. "Bob Hughes had to take his two ladders home. His wife told him he had to paint the garage this weekend or she was going to burn the thing down."

Nick put his paint roller down and wiped his hands on his worn jeans. "You don't need another ladder, Katie," he said with teasing lights in his dark brown eyes. "What you need is longer legs."

"Very amusing, Nick." She made a face at him

as he dropped down to his knees in front of her. "What is this? Your Toulouse-Lautrec impersonation?"

"Sit on my shoulders."

"You've got to be kidding." The mere thought of sitting on those broad shoulders had her tingling in places she'd forgotten she had. Her heart rate picked up a beat.

"No. Climb on. Weren't you a cheerleader in high school?"

"No."

"Well, I was. Climb on." He motioned impatiently for her to follow his instructions. "What are you? Chicken?"

"You said the magic words, Nick," Darrell Baylor said, laughing at Katie's suddenly determined expression. "Nobody ever dared Katie Quaid and got away with it."

Against her better judgment Katie eased herself onto Nick's shoulders, her roller clutched in her right hand. The fingers of her left hand threaded into his thick black hair as he rose carefully, his muscles bunching and straining beneath her. "If you drop me, Leone, you're going to have a bald spot."

"I wouldn't dream of dropping you, kitten."

The endearment raised a few eyebrows among Katie's longtime friends and brought a blush to Katie's cheeks, though she had to admit she didn't mind Nick having a pet name for her. It struck her as odd, because she usually found pet names to be somehow demeaning or insulting. But coming from Nick it didn't sound that way at all. She felt closer to him, and that was definitely what she wanted.

She tried to concentrate on painting, but it was difficult while sitting on Nick's shoulders with Nick hanging on to her ankles. More than once he let one hand wander up to her knee to tickle her there or snuck his fingers under the hem of her jeans to tickle her calf. She retaliated by squirming around until he got a crick in his neck and had to set her down.

Working side by side with his new neighbors Nick told them about growing up working in the construction industry. As a teenager he had spent summers working for his father, a carpenter, and his uncle Guido, the bricklayer.

"My old man found out early on I was better at hitting my thumb with the hammer than hitting the nail. Everyone was a lot happier when I took up cooking."

"I know my wife will be glad," Darrell said, wiping some paint from his hand on the leg of his overalls. "Zoe is wild for Italian food."

"What am I wild for?" Zoe asked, coming into the room with her two children trailing behind her.

"His body," Katie said teasingly. She ducked the rag Darrell tossed at her.

"Dream on, darlin'," Zoe said dryly, rolling her large dark eyes as she sent her husband a loving smile.

Reese charged across the room to his father. "Let me paint, Daddy!"

Little Charisse, the younger of the two Baylor children, ran after her brother, tears brimming in her eyes when she realized Daddy could only hold one of them up to help paint the wall. Without the slightest hesitation, Nick scooped her up.

"Here you go, sweetheart. You can help me paint."

Charisse eyed him warily over her shoulder, then accepted the roller with both hands and went to work, evidently satisfied this stranger was okay because he was working next to her daddy.

"I don't know if that's wise, Nick," Zoe said in a warning tone. Dressed for her shift at the hospital, she automatically stepped out of the range of splattering paint. "She'll get more paint on you than she will on the wall."

"That's okay." Nick grinned. He tickled the little girl with his free hand. "We're doing just great, aren't we, honey?"

Charisse shrieked in delight and smacked the paint-soaked roller against the wall, sending a shower of tiny blue specks into Nick's face. Only the children were painting as everyone else nearly doubled over laughing—everyone except Katie, who had become unusually quiet.

He was unquestionably good with children. But that didn't have anything to do with the two of them, Katie told herself. She managed a smile as she reached out and wiped a smudge of paint from Charisse's pudgy cheek.

"You're a good sport, Nick," Zoe said, tossing him a clean rag to wipe the paint off. "You must really like children."

"What? Are you joking? I don't like kids, I love

'em," he said, gently wrapping his big hand around Charisse's tiny ones to help her move the roller in the proper manner. "Someday I'll have a dozen."

"Now don't you go doing anything stupid. You hear me, Katie Marie?" Maggie called toward Katie's bedroom as she toed off her sneakers.

Katie emerged in a pink jogging suit, her long dark hair pulled back into a simple ponytail. She took the jumbo plastic bottle of diet cola from her friend and headed for the kitchen with her wolfhound tagging along behind her.

"I'm sure I don't know what you mean," she said.

Maggie scowled. She plunked a rented movie down on the VCR and went to the kitchen, stuffing her hands into the pockets of the long black cardigan she wore over an oversized yellow T-shirt. "I mean something stupid such as not seeing Nick anymore just because of a careless remark."

"I'm not doing that," Katie said. She tossed a bag of popcorn into the microwave oven and punched the appropriate buttons. She pulled a chew treat out of a drawer and gave it to her dog, watching him wander off to flop down on his pillow behind the couch.

There was no point in talking about how she'd felt that afternoon—hurt, empty, filled with a longing she knew was pointless. How many times had she felt the same mix of emotions in the last five years? Hundreds. Probably thousands. For a long, long time after her accident she had felt them every day. Then she had struggled to push those feelings out of her life until they only haunted her on special occasions—Christmas, the announcement of a friend's pregnancy, the birthdays of friends' children. She wasn't going to discuss those feelings now, nor was she about to let them interfere with her decision to have a relationship with Nick.

"You're not?" Maggie eyed her suspiciously.

"No." Katie selected two tall glasses from the cupboard, slipped behind Maggie to the refrigerator to pull out a tray of ice cubes, and plunked three into each glass. Maggie never took her eyes off Katie as she watched her open the pop bottle and pour equal measures of the fizzing liquid into each glass. "Nick and I are going to the concert in the park tomorrow."

"You are?"

"Yes. What movie did you get?"

Maggie planted her hands on her narrow waist and looked disgusted. "I came over here prepared to give you a big speech. Now you tell me I don't need to. Do I get an explanation?"

Katie took the popcorn out of the microwave, grabbed her glass, and headed for the living room with Maggie right on her heels. They settled on the Chippendale love seat.

"I'm sorry I spoiled your big moment, Mary Margaret," Katie said dryly, propping her stockinged feet on the low cherry butler's table and reaching for the TV remote control on the end table beside her. "I've decided I want to go on seeing Nick. We enjoy each other's company. If things start looking serious, I'll have to tell him about . . . everything. Then he can decide for himself. In the meantime I plan to enjoy myself," she said with a smile that didn't quite erase all the worry from her eyes.

"Good for you." Maggie's look still held traces of suspicion, but she dropped the subject.

They sat back to watch an old Tracy-Hepburn movie, but Katie's thoughts were elsewhere. She was postponing telling Nick about her accident. Reasons for and against that decision battled inside her. To tell him now could be premature; they hadn't been seeing each other for long. Putting it off was giving her more time to enjoy being with him, because there was every chance he would want to break it off when she told him. On the other hand, waiting was selfish. Waiting was dangerous. What if she waited too long?

The trick was going to be in the timing. No one knew better than Katie how important timing was. A split second's miscalculation had cost her her dream of a place on the United States equestrian team, her dream of a career in riding, her dream of children of her own. Bad timing had nearly cost her her life. This time it could cost her her heart.

"I could have picked you up," Nick said, easing a bottle of white wine into the wicker picnic basket on his kitchen table.

"It's a beautiful day. We'll enjoy the walk," Katie said brightly. "Besides, I think you picked me up yesterday enough to last me."

He turned and tapped a finger against the end of her nose. "Cute." Looking down at the enormous gray dog sitting at Katie's feet, he said, "You could have thrown a saddle on him and ridden him."

He tossed the wolfhound a piece of cheddar cheese, then turned back to his packing, adding beige linen napkins in silver rings, and a container holding two generous wedges of cheesecake.

"Are you planning to feed everyone at the concert?" Katie asked. She'd patiently stood and watched him pack cold chicken, a container of pasta salad, a plate of cheeses, a bunch of green grapes, a small loaf of Italian bread, and a box of crackers.

"Fine wine and fine food to go with fine music," he said smugly. Taking her completely by surprise, he turned and gave her a smacking kiss on the lips. "Ain't you got no class, lady?"

Katie giggled as she dropped her dog's leash and ran her hands up Nick's chest to his shoulders. She raised up on tiptoe and brushed her lips against his.

Nick didn't question his good fortune. He slid his arms around Katie and lifted her against him as he took command of the kiss. She tasted like springtime—fresh and sweet—and smelled like a bouquet. She was so soft and giving against him, all he could think of was carrying her across the hall to his bedroom, taking off her pretty summer dress, and making love to her until they were both exhausted. His body responded as if that were exactly the plan for the day—until Watch intruded.

The wolfhound wedged his long nose between them and whined.

Katie dropped back on her heels, laughing at the disgruntled expression Nick wore.

"Your brother trained him to do that, didn't he?" Nick asked in an accusing tone. "He's not attack trained, he's breaking-up-lovers trained."

A secret smile stole across Katie's lips as she knelt and hugged her dog. Lovers. That word had a nice, warm ring to it on a spring day full of promise. Doubts and fears didn't belong at a picnic in the park. Katie had determinedly left them at home.

"He's just jealous," she said, scratching Watch behind his silky ears. The scent of lavender clung to the dog from his weekly bath. "You don't mind my bringing him along, do you? He loves concerts in the park."

"I don't mind, as long he knows you are my date and he's just a shaggy chaperon."

When Nick started straightening the kitchen, Katie asked if there was anything she could do to help.

"Yeah. There's a blanket on my bed we can take to sit on. Why don't you get it?"

His room looked no different than it had the first time she'd seen it. It looked like a cyclone had hit and left no survivors. There was a pillow on the floor beside a copy of *Gourmet* magazine and a pair of running shoes. The door wore a different assortment of shirts hung in all the same places as before. There were jeans slung over the back of a chair and a pile of mismatched socks on the seat. There were no pictures on the walls, no curtains at the window, only a cracked, yellowed shade. Katie shook her head fondly as she searched the jumbled bed for the blanket. The first thing she picked up turned out to be a cape.

A cape? A beautiful black satin cape with gold silk lining. How odd, she thought.

"What's this?"

Nick turned. His heart went to his throat and lodged there. "A . . . it's a . . ."

"Cape," Katie supplied the word for him, too preoccupied with the garment to notice the look of panic on Nick's face.

"Right!" He thought he had put it away. How could he have been so careless? His pulse pounded wildly as he tried to think up a reasonable explanation. Thank God she hadn't found any part of his costume that was harder to explain than this one. A cape was bad enough, but a black satin G-string would be next to impossible.

Katie frowned as she slung the cape over her shoulders and looked at the way the hem dragged the ground. "It's a man's cape," she said.

"Yeah . . . it's a . . . a . . . something else I found in the attic." His words came out sounding more like a question than an answer, but then that went well with his expression. He looked as if he were a teenager who'd been caught out after curfew without a legitimate excuse.

"It's in awfully good shape," Katie remarked, running the luscious fabric through her hands.

"It...was...in a trunk." That much was true. He'd packed all his Highwayman gear in a trunk and thought never to take it out again, until that toad of a county engineer had shown up with his demand for a new curb and gutter.

It occurred to Nick he had a perfect opportunity to tell Katie the whole truth. He had no intention of doing that, however. He was off balance now, and somehow, the timing seemed wrong. Here was Katie Quaid, proper and elegant in her stylish spring dress, with her wolfhound at her side and her hair done up in a classic chignon, out for an afternoon of Mozart in the park. Nick got the feeling an erotic dancer from New Jersey wouldn't quite fit in.

He was being an out-and-out coward. He accepted that. He didn't mind being a coward for a while longer if it meant spending more time with Katie. He would tell her. Soon. He just wanted to make sure the timing was right. As a dancer and a gourmet chef he knew timing was everything. It could mean the difference between a perfect rou-

tine and a sloppy one. It could mean the difference between a culinary triumph and a disaster. In
this case it could mean the difference between
building a solid relationship with Katie and losing her.

FIVE

"ARE YOU SURE this is what you want to do for your birthday, Maggie?" Katie asked, unable to keep the apprehension out of her voice. "Wouldn't you rather go to a five-star restaurant and eat yourself sick?"

"No." Maggie took her gaze off the traffic long enough to shoot her friend an irrepressible grin. "I'd rather go to Hepplewhite's and stare at gorgeous men until my eyes fall out. What's the matter, Katie? You should be immune to gorgeous men after all the time you've spent looking at Nick these last few weeks."

Katie squirmed on the passenger side of the front seat. She already was feeling embarrassed, and they hadn't even gotten to the nightclub yet. "When I see Nick, he's got clothes on."

"Now, that is a shame," Zoe said, leaning toward the front seat as far as her seat belt would allow. "Nick Leone is one fine-looking man, honey. The men at Hepplewhite's would probably look ordinary next to him."

Maggie changed lanes, scooting her car to the front of the pack on the highway. "I can safely say I wouldn't mind watching Nick do a little striptease."

"Mag-gie!" Katie said with a groan. She dropped her head back against the seat and stared at the roof.

"Don't be such a prude."

"I'm not a prude. We're going to pay money to watch men take their clothes off—I'm embarrassed."

"That's half the fun of going to one of these clubs," Zoe said. "We women can act as silly and wild and embarrassed as we want to."

Katie glanced back over the seat, her gray eyes wide with curiosity. "You've been to one of these places before?"

"Once, about two years ago. It was a blast. The men were terrific dancers. They could have left all their clothes on and still the show would have been worth the price of admission. One man in particular brought the house down. He did his whole act wearing a black silk mask tied across his eyes, so you never truly got to see who he was. Lord, he had the most beautiful body!" She rolled her eyes and nearly swooned at the memory. "And dance? That boy could have put Baryshnikov to shame."

Hepplewhite's, Katie discovered, was no sleazy strip joint. It was a large, lavishly decorated nightclub in a suburb of Washington. The air was filled with music, laughter, and excitement. Women of every description had come there for one reason—to have fun. It was a party atmosphere, and the party began shortly after Katie, Maggie, and Zoe claimed seats at a table near the stage.

The first act was a dapper gentleman in a top hat and tails who did a clever routine to "Putting on the Ritz." Maggie and Zoe were on the edges of their seats, cheering. Katie kept her hand ready to cover her eyes when things got too steamy. As his routine neared the end, she was certain he was going to end up wearing nothing but his top hat and spats. She was all ready to hide her eyes, when Maggie grabbed her hand.

"For heaven's sake, Katie! They don't take everything off! Some things are best left to the imagination."

Katie slumped back in her chair, weak with relief. "Thank heaven."

It wasn't that she was so straitlaced, it was just that Katie hadn't had a lot of opportunities in her life to see naked men. Having them dance up to her was more than she was ready for.

When she had been a teenager and her friends had been discovering the wonderful world of the opposite sex, Katie had been too scrawny to capture any young man's attention and too wrapped up in her riding to care. After her accident she had steered clear of men in general. Now they were parading around in front of her, taking their clothes off!

She had to admit, though, Maggie and Zoe had been right. Hepplewhite's was a fun place. It seemed to her that the men who were dancing were enjoying themselves as much as were the ladies watching them. Katie had seen strip joints portrayed in the movies as dark, smoky rooms crowded with men who sat and leered while some bored, cynical woman undressed for them. Hepplewhite's was so far removed from her preconceived image, it seemed innocent in comparison. By the fourth act she had relaxed enough to clap along in time with the music as a blond "cowboy" danced for them.

She caught herself comparing each of the dancers with Nick. None of them was as handsome or well built, in Katie's opinion. He probably could have danced circles around them. She thought back to the day he had helped out at the Drewes mansion and how he had teased her by saying he had been a male stripper. She was going to have to tell him he was eminently qualified.

"It's him!" Zoe said excitedly. Her gaze was riveted to the stage as the headline act of the evening appeared. She pressed her hands to her breast. "Be still my heart. It's the Highwayman!"

He was dressed all in black, from his hat to his gleaming boots. A mask of black silk hid his face. He drew his cape around him as he took center stage and command of the audience with one burning look. A hush fell over the crowd. Then, with a flick of his wrist, his hat sailed out into the room, and the show was on.

The music was fast and driving. The Highwayman never missed a beat. He was brilliant, spinning and leaping, twirling the black satin cape until it seemed as if it were a living thing. He slid it from his broad shoulders and snapped it and waved it and made it dance like a matador's cape before he dropped it to the floor.

Katie was mesmerized. Now she knew what Nick had meant when he said dancing was the ultimate combination of art and athleticism. She couldn't take her eyes off the Highwayman, couldn't let herself blink for fear she would miss something. His dancing was powerful and beautiful, the way she had imagined Nick's would be. He moved with strength and agility, speed and grace.

The more she stared at him, the more she realized he was built like Nick. As he shed his black shirt he revealed hard, broad shoulders and a trim waist. The rippling play of muscle over bone, skin over muscle, fascinated Katie. The ridges of muscle across his stomach made her breath catch as he rolled his hip in time to the sensuous, throbbing beat.

The music never slowed. Nor did the Highwayman. Gradually he bared a body that should have been cast in bronze. To see that body only intensified the strength and elegance of the dance. To be unable to see the face behind the mask only intensified the air of romance and mystery. For the first time this evening Katie couldn't wait to see the dancer up close.

"He's coming this way!" Maggie looked as if she were ready to explode from excitement. She was bouncing on her chair like a jumping bean.

It sounded as if Zoe was hyperventilating, but Katie couldn't bring herself to look. She couldn't take her eyes off the dark, handsome stranger who was moving their way in a series of sinuous twists and turns. As he drew near she thought it was remarkable how much his body resembled Nick's—the way his chest tapered to his waist, the way his belly button wasn't quite centered, and the way that mole sat just to the right of it, the mole that was shaped like a crouching bunny.

Katie's shocked gaze shot up into the equally

shocked gaze of the Highwayman. They went pale simultaneously. It *was* Nick!

He was on the other side of the room in a flash; then his act was over, and he vanished from the stage behind a sudden cloud of smoke.

Now she had some idea what it felt like to fall off a cliff, Katie thought. Her stomach seemed to be somewhere in the vicinity of her ankles. She felt as if she'd just let go of a live wire. With a shaking hand she raised her glass to her lips and took a long drink of white wine, hoping it would steady her nerves.

Nick *was* an erotic dancer. He hadn't been kidding when he'd told her. He wasn't just any erotic dancer either. He was the headline act at one of the hottest nightclubs on the East Coast. He was the Highwayman, the act every woman in the room had been waiting for with her heart pounding in her breast in anticipation. Nick, who in some ways seemed so shy, was moonlighting in a G-string!

The wild applause and cheers of the crowd began to penetrate Katie's stunned brain. What if Maggie and Zoe had recognized him? What would she say to them? They would want to know why she hadn't told them Nick was the famous Highwayman.

Why hadn't Nick told her himself? She didn't count the time he had tried to tell her at the Drewes mansion because she hadn't taken him seriously and he'd known it. There had been plenty of opportunities for him to try to tell her again. Obviously the cape she had found on his bed the day of the concert in the park was the same cape he had worked so expertly tonight. Why hadn't she recognized that cape? More to the point, why hadn't he explained all this to her when she had found it?

She couldn't decide whether she should feel angry, hurt, embarrassed, or all three. One thing she was certain of: Nick was going to get a piece of her mind when she saw him.

"Wasn't he wonderful?" Zoe was panting as if she had danced every step of the performance with him. "Didn't I tell y'all he was gorgeous?"

"Gorgeous? Sugar, the word doesn't even come close to describing him!" Maggie fell back in her chair, fanning her flushed face with a limp cocktail napkin. She shook her head in amazement. "Not even Nick has a body that perfect."

Katie's dark brows drew together in annoyance. Nick did too have a body that perfect. Part of her wanted to tell them so. She was proud of Nick, she realized with no small amount of astonishment. He was a marvelously talented dancer. The fact that he stripped to his skivvies—well, even less—as he performed didn't enter into it. The fact that hundreds of women got to stare at his beautiful body as he danced was of no consequence.

The hell it wasn't, Katie thought as she took another drink of her wine. The idea of all these women getting to see what Nick hid under his clothes was distinctly disturbing to her. The fact of the matter was, she was jealous. It was the first time in her life she had ever felt that way about a man. The sensation was a little frightening and strangely invigorating.

A stand-up comedian had come out onstage to do her act while the crowd and the dancers caught their collective breath. Katie didn't even try to focus her attention on the woman. She had so many things on her mind, she ignored the raucous laughter of the crowd, and she ignored the waiter at her side who was trying to slip her a piece of paper.

Unobtrusively he tucked a folded note into her hand as if he had had much practice at the secretive move. "One of our gentlemen asked me to give this to you," he whispered.

"Thank you." She opened the note in her lap. It was barely legible. The handwriting was bold, hurried, and messy—the way Nick wrote when he wasn't wearing his glasses. Either he wanted her to meet him backstage, or he wanted her to beat the backstop. She tucked the note into her skirt pocket and turned to Zoe, who was all wrapped up in the jokes the comic was telling. "I'm going to step out for a breath of fresh air."

Zoe lifted a hand in acknowledgment and nodded absently.

Katie let the waiter lead her around the fringe of the crowd to a door marked Employees Only. He knocked twice. The door was pulled back a crack. A hand reached out and pulled Katie to the other side, into a hallway where fluorescent light glared off white walls.

Nick leaned back against a wall and shoved his hands into the pockets of his dark green robe. His hair fell onto his forehead in damp, gleaming curls. A white towel was slung around his neck. He looked impossibly virile, but Katie tried to ignore that.

"Nick Leone, you have got a lot of explaining to do." She jabbed a slender finger in the direction of his breastbone but stopped short of touching him. Nick looked down at her with brown eyes that were at once apologetic and apprehensive.

"I know," he said, wincing at the censure in her voice. "I'm sorry, honey. I meant to tell you. I tried to tell you a hundred times, a million times—"

"You never quite got the job done."

"The timing always seemed wrong."

A door opened to his right, and one of the other dancers emerged. Katie recognized him as the cowboy who had danced earlier. He was blond and tan and wearing nothing but a towel hitched around his lean hips and a sexy grin. "Great job tonight, Nick."

"Thanks, Derek." He turned back to Katie, who had squeezed her eyes shut and was blushing like a bride.

"Isn't there somewhere more private where we

can discuss this?" she asked through clenched teeth. She had seen enough scantily clad men to last her for a while.

Nick crossed the hall and knocked on the door of Jack Clark's office. He stuck his head inside. "Jack, can I borrow your office for a few minutes?"

The manager of Hepplewhite's glanced up from his paperwork. "Sure, Nick."

Determined to be annoyed with him, Katie frowned as Nick took her by the elbow and ushered her into the office. A handsome, dark-haired man stubbed out a slender cigar in a crystal ashtray and stood up behind the desk.

"Katie, this is Jack Clark, the manager of Hepplewhite's. Jack, this is Kathryn Quaid."

"It's a pleasure to meet you, Ms. Quaid," Clark said smoothly as he moved toward the door. "Are you enjoying the show tonight?"

"Oh"—Katie gave him a wavering smile—"it's been quite an evening."

Jack chuckled. "We'll take that as a compliment. If you'll excuse me, I'll let you two have a little privacy."

"Thanks, Jack," Nick said, mentally bracing himself for what was liable to happen as soon as the door closed behind his boss.

Never in his wildest dreams had he imagined Katie would show up at Hepplewhite's. Katie liked going to the movies, a quiet dinner, a leisurely walk in the park. She wasn't at all the night-on-the-town type. When he'd danced up to her table and looked down into those stunned gray eyes, he had felt as if the floor had suddenly dropped out from under his feet. "Katie, what are you doing here?"

"What am *I* doing here?" she said, incredulous. She paced an imaginary line on the deep red carpet a few feet away from Nick, her hands planted on her slim hips. "I would ask you what *you* are doing here, but it was pretty self-explanatory."

"I tried to tell you before," he said in his own defense. He couldn't placate his own conscience with that flimsy excuse, and he was certain Katie wasn't going to be impressed by it. "I really did, but I'm not always good with words. I didn't know how to explain it to you. I was afraid you wouldn't understand."

"This was what you meant when you said you were going to be working for a friend a couple of nights a week, wasn't it? This is how you're making back the money you had to spend on the curb and gutter, isn't it?" she asked, putting all the pieces of the puzzle together in her mind.

"Yes."

"This is why you never want to tell anybody about your past, isn't it? You'd rather let people think you were a spy or a jewel thief than tell them the truth. You're ashamed to tell them you're a stripper."

"Erotic dancer," he corrected her, anger lighting fires in his dark eyes. "I'm not ashamed of it. I'm proud of being a dancer. I think I do a damn good job. The reason I didn't want to tell anybody was because I didn't think they'd understand. I guess I was right, huh, Katie? You don't understand. You're the one who's ashamed. You're ashamed of me."

"I am not!" Katie insisted, squaring off with him toe to toe, not the least intimidated by his towering height or the glower he wore, which made him look as ruthless as any mercenary. "I'll thank you to stop putting words in my mouth, Nick Leone. I thought you were wonderful. I thought you were magnificent—and that was before I knew it was you!"

"You—" Her words penetrated his anger, and he caught himself in midtirade, his expression softening from one of hurt and fury to one of stunned surprise. "You thought I was wonderful?"

"Yes," Katie said, relaxing as the fight drained out of her. "Your dance was so powerful, so elegant. The part where you spun around and around with the cape waving above your head took my breath away."

"You liked that part? I've been thinking of changing that," he said in a conversational tone of voice.

"Oh, no, don't change it. It was riveting." Suddenly Katie pressed her hands to her temples and shook her head in amazement. "I can't believe we're having this conversation. I can't believe my Nick, who won't put his glasses on in public, is the same man who flung his clothes into a sea of screaming women."

A delighted smile split his dark face. He felt a little flutter in the vicinity of his heart. "*Your* Nick?"

Katie's cheeks bloomed as pink as her skirt. "A figure of speech," she muttered, staring down at her shoes.

Nick stepped behind her and slid his arms around her waist. He dipped his head down to nuzzle her ear, and murmured, "I like it."

"Do you?" Tingles ran over every inch of her body. She had a hard time keeping her mind on the conversation and off thoughts of the way his muscles had gleamed under the stage lights and the way his hips had undulated so seductively as he had danced to her table.

"Very much," he whispered in a silky voice. He ran his lips down the column of her throat and back up as his hands splayed across her tummy, and pressed her back into the heat of his body.

When Katie closed her eyes she could see the rippling of his hard abdominal muscles and the trickle of sweat that had trailed down the line of ebony hair on his belly as he had performed. She could feel the thick sexual tension that had filled the air as he had moved as sleek and powerful as a jaguar, every eye in the place on him.

She twisted around, lifting her mouth to Nick's, demanding his kiss, giving him free entry to the sweet warmth beyond her lips. When he raised his head and sighed, she looked up at him with her heart in her eyes and whispered, "How could you ever think I'd be ashamed of you?"

The sharp, firm edges of his lips twisted into a wry smile. He ran a finger down her dainty nose. "You're so prim and proper, such a Southern lady, I wasn't so sure you'd have room in your life for a stripper from Jersey."

"Erotic dancer," she corrected with a tender smile. She lifted her hand to the lean, hard plane of his cheek. He was so tough, so masculine, yet the look in his velvet brown eyes was one of uncertainty and hope. It won him yet another corner of Katie's heart. In the back of her mind she realized there weren't many corners left. Nick was going to own the whole thing soon. Whether or not she was being very smart about the situation she couldn't decide, but it certainly felt right.

"After your act, when everybody was cheering

and applauding, I wanted to turn to Maggie and Zoe and tell them it was you because I was so proud of you."

"You did?" His eyes twinkled as he turned her hand and pressed a kiss to her palm. Her hand was so tiny and feminine in his, the contrast made his stomach tighten.

Katie nodded. From the spot he'd kissed a shiver ran up her arm and spread through her, teasing all her nerve endings into awareness. "And do you know what else I felt when I heard all that clapping and screaming?"

"What?" The word was no more than an exhalation of the breath that had caught in his lungs as he gazed down at her.

"Jealous," she whispered, still a little amazed herself.

"Jealous? You were jealous?" he asked, looking extremely pleased with this tidbit of information.

With an embarrassed smile she nodded again. "I didn't like the idea of all those strange women drooling over your body."

Nick could hardly contain his elation. He

wanted to let out a war whoop and dance around the office. He had been so afraid Katie wouldn't understand, that she'd want to walk away from him when she found out about his dancing. Instead he was getting admissions from her that he had hoped for but hadn't expected to hear for quite a while.

He was ready to take steps toward a more serious relationship with her, but he had sensed—and respected—Katie's hesitancy. He knew she wasn't one to let a man get too close too quickly. It was her reluctance that had won her the title Ice Princess from men who hadn't been patient enough to earn her trust. She was giving him now a huge victory when he had braced himself for utter defeat.

"But they don't know it's me," he pointed out to her. "Only you know it's me behind the mask."

"That's right." She smiled, pleased to know she was the only woman who had unmasked the elusive Highwayman.

Running his hands back from her face, over her satiny dark hair, Nick gave her a look burning with sensual promise. "I wouldn't mind giving you a private performance sometime."

"Oh?" The word quivered on Katie's lips as erotic images of Nick dancing just for her filled her head. She could feel her bones melting to the consistency of butter on a hot stove, and leaned gratefully into Nick's strength as he bent and kissed her again.

Need surged through his body, followed by a groan that came from the depths of his soul. "I'd give you one right now if this weren't a borrowed office." He lifted her hand and slipped it inside his robe, pressing it to his chest so she could feel his heart thudding under his ribs.

"Feel what you do to me, Katie," he demanded. He ran his hand down her back and over the delicious curve of her bottom, and drew her against him so she could feel his need not only beneath her hand but straining urgently against her belly. "I care about you so much. I want you so much, Katie."

His words set off an avalanche of trembling inside her. He wanted her. She wanted him. Oh, how she wanted him! Katie had never known such need before—the need to hold and cherish and express her feelings in a purely physical way, the need to have a man want all those same things with her in his arms. However, this wasn't the time or the place. Any minute Jack Clark was going to want his office back. Then there was still the matter of her own secret.

Nick could feel her pull back from him slightly—emotionally as well as physically. He wrapped his arms around her and held her close, banishing the physical distance. "I know you're not ready for that step yet, kitten. I won't push it. But when you are ready, I'll be here, and I'll want you just as much as I want you right now."

She looked up at him with misty eyes and a smile as soft as dew. Another corner of her heart went to him gladly. Aside from his daring her to kiss him that first time, Nick hadn't pressured her in any way. His patience had done wonders in helping her relax with him and with the idea of gradually entering into a more physical relationship with him. No other man she'd known had possessed his patience. "Thank you for understanding," she whispered.

He smiled against her lips, falling a little more in love with her for letting him see her vulnerability, then he made a little face at her and asked, "Now, just what are you doing here, Katie Quaid?"

"It was Maggie's idea," she explained, feeling like a schoolgirl who'd gotten caught at a wild party. It was all she could do to keep from giggling. "This is what she wanted to do to celebrate her birthday."

"I should have guessed Maggie would be behind it," he said with a chuckle. "Is she having a good time?"

"What a silly question!" Katie laughed. "As my brother would say, she's in hog heaven. So is Zoe."

"What about you?" he asked, tickling her. "Are you enjoying yourself, Katie?"

She squirmed in his arms but didn't try to escape. It was more fun to snuggle against him. "More than I had thought I would. I didn't have any idea what it would be like. It's a lot of fun. You guys are fantastic dancers."

"Thanks," he said, thanking heaven Katie

was more open-minded than he had given her credit for.

"How did you get started?" she asked.

Nick let go of her and leaned back against the edge of the desk. "When I was trying to get discovered in New York, I found out there are a lot of good dancers but not many jobs. You have to be more than just a good dancer to make it on Broadway. I finally saw I didn't have the extra something and decided to set my sights on my other dream—the restaurant. But I needed money to make that dream come true. I heard the manager of a club was auditioning men for a high-class erotic show and figured why not? They wanted top dancers with imaginative acts to provide fun, escapist entertainment for ladies. The pay was high, and it sounded like I'd have a good time."

"And the Highwayman was born," Katie finished the story for him.

"You got it." He reached out and caught her hand, just because he wanted to touch her. It seemed as if he never stopped wanting to touch Katie. "I gained a reputation, toured up and down the East Coast for two years until I had enough money for the down payment on the building I wanted. When that curb and gutter problem came up, this was the quickest way I knew of to get the money. Jack had made me a standing offer to come back anytime I wanted."

"How long are you going to have to work here?"

"Two shows a night, two nights a week until the restaurant opens. Do you mind?"

"I mind that you have to work so hard. You're working day and night on your building, helping out at the Drewes mansion, and working here too."

Nick smiled gently at the look of concern in her big gray eyes. He drew her into his arms and kissed her lightly. "Don't worry, kitten. Mama always said I had more energy than any ten kids. I can handle it and still have time left on my dance card for you."

He glanced at the clock on the desk and sighed. "Right now I have to get ready for my next show."

Katie slid her arms around his neck and gave him a long, thorough kiss. When she finished, she stepped back and winked at him. "Knock 'em dead, Yankee."

Nick grinned. Their relationship had survived the unmasking of his secret identity. The optimist in him predicted it would be smooth sailing from then on.

SIX

"So what's he like? Is he a nice guy or a jerk or what?" Nick asked, wishing he could watch Katie's gray eyes for her answers. He could sense the complexity of emotions in her as they drove west out of Briarwood on a climbing, winding road. She finally was taking him to meet her brother, who, according to rumor, was something of a hermit. Maggie had described him as impossible, cantankerous, and arrogant—and Nick was pretty sure she had a crush on the guy. He couldn't wait to meet Rylan Quaid.

"Rylan?" Katie rolled her eyes. "He's like a giant prickly pear: all spiny on the outside and soft on the inside. He's a tyrant. He's stubborn and owly and—"

"—and you love him," Nick finished with a grin.

Katie smiled in return. Only Nick could have made that determination from what she had said. Sometimes he was too perceptive. She wondered if he picked up similar notes in her voice when she spoke of him, because what she was feeling for Nick these days was love, or at least the beginnings of it. She had realized it the night at Hepplewhite's over a week ago, the night she had discovered his secret identity. Since then, scarcely an hour had gone by that she hadn't thought about her feelings for him.

She had been fretting for days about taking Nick to meet Ry. Ry was so overprotective of her. He had called her several times since word had reached his ears that his baby sister was going out with a man with a mysterious past. It had taken every threat Katie could think of to keep her brother from paying Nick a visit.

She had deliberately put off introducing them until rumors about Nick had died down and until

Nick had established several good friendships with people she knew Ry respected. She wanted him to like Nick, but knew she would go on seeing Nick with or without her brother's blessing.

They rode in silence for a while. Instead of turning on the air conditioner to cool the warm spring air, Nick kept his window rolled down so he could drink in the rich scents of the Virginia countryside.

"Don't let him intimidate you," Katie said suddenly.

Nick lifted an eyebrow. "Intimidate me?" She was talking about her brother the way she might talk about a Doberman.

"The idea won't sound so strange to you once you've met him."

They turned in at a gravel drive that twisted up and around a hill so wooded, barely a drop of sunlight spilled through the canopy of green overhead. When they emerged from the trees at the top of the hill, pastures rolled before them like an emerald carpet. Sturdy, four-plank oak fencing marked one field from the next, separated one group of horses from another. The sign at the end of the first field read simply Quaid Farm.

"They're beautiful!" Nick said in awe as he slowed his sports car to a crawl. "When you said you grew up on a farm, I thought of pigs and cows and tractors and stuff. You never said anything about horses. What kind are they? Thoroughbreds?"

"Some of them," Katie replied. "Some are Hanoverians, imported from Germany. We're experimenting with a crossbreeding program to combine the speed and agility of the Thoroughbred with the size and superior temperament of the Hanoverian. They make excellent show jumpers."

"We?" Nick questioned, more than a little impressed with her answer.

"I inherited part of the farm when Daddy died."

She didn't tell him that she had tried to give it to Ry after her accident. She had so loved riding that when the doctors had told her she could never ride again, her first instinct had been to get completely away from it. To own part of the farm meant she had to express an interest in it. To drive down these lanes and walk through the stables knowing she could never get nearer than an arm's length away from these animals that had been the largest part of her life for seventeen years had been too painful to bear.

Ry had stubbornly refused to take her offer, however. Not only that, he had bullied her into becoming more involved in the management of the farm while she had been recuperating. She had hated him for it at the time, but now she thanked him. Instead of isolating herself, she took great pride in the stock they raised and trained.

Nick parked the car near the first of two long, white stables painted with royal-blue trim. The big doors on either end of the building had been rolled back, exposing two rows of box stalls separated by a wide aisle. He killed the engine and glanced at Katie. "Do you ride?"

"I used to," she said, quickly unbuckling her seat belt and climbing out of the car, pulling the seat forward to let Watch out of the back. She already had decided this would be the day she would tell Nick. She had brought him there to do so. But she wanted to wait until they were alone and the moment was right.

She bypassed the office, heading down the wide aisle of the stable after Watch, who jogged along with his nose to the concrete floor. Nick danced along behind her, trying to take it all in at once—the oak walls and iron bars of the big box stalls, the smell of wood shavings and hay and horses, the sounds that echoed through the long building. He darted back and forth between the rows of stalls like an eager boy, wanting to see each and every horse up close.

"Damn!" The shout came from beyond the far end of the stable. Tools and curses flew.

Nick stopped dead in his tracks. "Sounds like he's in a bad mood."

"He's always in a bad mood. Cease fire!" Katie called before stepping out of the building.

Nick took one look at Ry and knew instantly what Katie had meant about being intimidated. The man was six feet four if he was an inch, and he was built like a bull and looked as angry as one as he stood snarling and scowling at a blue and gray tractor. Sweat ran down his face and the sculpted muscles of his bare chest and abdomen, and had soaked into the waistband of his jeans. He wiped a hand across his forehead, slicking back his dark hair.

At a glance no one would have said this man

was related to little Katie. He was as huge and masculine as she was petite and feminine. There were similarities in their faces, however—the shape and color of their eyes, the high cheekbones, the expressive mouth, and stubborn chin.

"Can you take time out from your swearing to say hello to your baby sister?" Katie asked dryly.

"Hi, princess." Ry bent and pressed a kiss to her cheek, never taking his wary gaze off Nick.

Katie stepped back to make the introductions. "Nick, this is my foul-tempered brother, Rylan. Ry, meet Nick Leone."

Ry glanced at his palm and smeared grease off it and onto the leg of his jeans. He clasped Nick's hand in a death grip. Nick gritted his teeth and squeezed right back, knowing the only way to gain the man's respect was to match him step for step.

"If this is going to turn into a bone-crushing contest, I'm leaving," Katie said with a pointed look at her brother.

"It's a pleasure to meet you," Nick said. "Katie's told me a lot about you."

"Yeah," Ry said, unsmiling. "I've heard a lot about you too."

None of it good, by the tone of his voice, Nick thought.

"Why are you trying to dismember that poor machine?" Katie asked, more to divert her brother's attention than anything else. If she let Ry have his way, he'd give Nick the third degree. He'd have the thumbscrews out before dinnertime.

"Jeepers cripes, the stupid thing won't start for love or money, and I know damn well there's juice in the battery." He scowled at the tractor as if he could intimidate it into behaving.

"Well, I don't think you can beat it into submission," Katie said. "Why don't you stop being so cheap and stubborn and hire someone to fix it—someone who knows what he's doing."

Hands on his hips Rylan stared down at his sister with a look that would have wilted most women and a lot of men. Katie didn't budge. "I'm not cheap, I'm thrifty."

"You're so tight, you squeak," she said with a laugh.

"Maybe the starter solenoid is bad," Nick said, trying to get a better look at the tractor's engine. "We could pull it out and check it."

"You know something about tractors?" Ry asked with his typical skeptical look.

Nick shook his head. "No, but I have a brother who rebuilds classic cars. I used to help him out once in a while."

As the men became involved with the contrary machine, Katie leaned back against the sun-warmed wall of the stable and breathed a sigh of relief, murmuring a thank-you to the jewel-blue sky. Rylan was her brother and she loved him, but he was like a bomb that had to be carefully defused. The only things Rylan had patience with were animals. It was a huge relief to see him poking around the tractor with Nick in some kind of male-bonding ritual.

When the tractor had been thoroughly discussed and tinkered with, the three of them took a stroll back through the stables.

"Do you know anything about horses, Nick?" Ry asked, sliding back the heavy door to a box stall.

"I know which end runs under the finish line first," Nick said with a grin, stepping into the stall behind Katie's brother. Katie stayed in the doorway. "But I don't have to be an expert to know this is a beautiful animal."

The bay mare was huge, sleek, and exquisitely made. She stretched her long slender neck, nudging Nick's arm with her velvety nose, her limpid brown eyes alight with curiosity.

"Hang on to her halter," Ry ordered as he squatted down to take the bandage off the mare's left front leg. He shot a glance over his shoulder to see how the city boy handled the task and looked pleased when he saw Nick stroking the mare's neck with one hand as he held on to her with the other. "She decided to go through a fence instead of over it. Tore up her leg."

"Were you riding her when it happened?" Nick asked.

"No. Our trainer was on her. I like to ride, but my size is something of a hindrance when it comes to going over big fences."

Nick looked to Katie, who was leaning back against the door frame, staring at the big horse with a strangely wistful expression. "Did you ever ride in shows?" he asked her.

Ry's head shot up, his gaze riveting on his sister.

"I used to," Katie replied, butterflies taking

wing in her stomach as she realized the moment of truth was drawing near. She was betting heavily on Nick's sensitivity and understanding, but there was just enough doubt in her to make her heart pound a little harder. She pushed away from the door, stepping out into the aisle.

Ry stood and patted the horse's shoulder absently as he watched Katie wander to the end of the barn to pet the dogs that had gathered there to sun themselves. He glanced at the first man his sister had brought to the farm in five years.

"Did I say the wrong thing?" Nick asked, confused by the brief flash of panic he'd seen in Katie's eyes.

"I reckon you better ask Katie that question," Ry said quietly. "But before you do, let me tell you something. You break that little gal's heart, and you're gonna be in a world of hurt yourself, slick. Are we clear on that particular point?"

Nick stared right back into the steel-hard gaze of Rylan Quaid. "Like crystal," he said. "You didn't have to warn me though. Hurting Katie is the last thing I want to do."

Ry nodded slowly. "Then we'll get along just fine, you and me."

*   *   *

"I think he likes you," Katie said with a smile as they climbed the hill that overlooked the farm. She gave his hand a little squeeze to try to calm her jitters.

"How could you tell?" Nick couldn't decide if Ry had tolerated him or despised him.

"He didn't throw you out. He let you hold the mare's halter. Of course, that was a test." They reached the top of the hill, and Katie gestured at the view of the farm. "It's beautiful, isn't it?"

Nick let his gaze settle on her, on the way the wind played with the ends of her long hair and the hem of her blue peasant skirt. The sun brought out the color in her cheeks. "Yes," he said softly. "Beautiful is the word I would use."

Katie turned and found herself in his arms. It was where she wanted to be. For the moment she pushed the thoughts of what she needed to tell Nick to the back of her mind. She needed to tell him, too, that she loved being in his arms, that she needed the feel of his mouth on hers. She drank in his kiss, memorizing the warm, silky texture of his tongue stroking hers, memorizing the way her breasts tingled as they flattened against his chest.

He pulled her down to the ground with him, gently laying her back but never breaking the kiss. His fingers quickly dispensed with the buttons on her cotton blouse and found her breasts. His blood flowed like fire in his veins as he felt her nipple bud beneath his thumb. Need tore through him.

The instant Nick's mouth closed over her breast, Katie was lost. She felt as if she were a beginner in the deep end of the swimming pool—drowning in sensation but not wanting to be saved. She had ignored her own sexuality for so long, now it was overwhelming her, sweeping away caution and sanity. She arched her back and bit into her lip as Nick sucked at her breast until it felt as if every nerve in her body were centered there. Her fingers dove into the thick silk of his hair, anchoring him in place as she moved restlessly beneath him, wanting more, wanting everything he could give her, wanting to give him everything in return.

Her responsiveness was fuel to the fire raging inside Nick. He had held back, waiting until Katie was ready to take the next step in their relationship, trying to content himself with hot kisses and cold showers. Suddenly contentment and waiting were the last things on his mind. He wanted to make love to her there, in the soft, sweet-smelling grass, with the sun burning down on his back and the breeze cooling the sweat on their skin.

Nick's hand stole beneath Katie's skirt. He stroked her soft inner thigh, snuck his fingers under the leg of her panties and found her warm and moist, as ready for him as he was for her. He held his breath against the surge in his loins as he eased a finger up inside her and listened to her whimper her pleasure and her need. Kissing her as deeply as he could, he stroked her and teased her until he thought he would burst from wanting her.

"Let's get this skirt off you, kitten," he whispered in a voice rough with desire. "I want to see you when we make love."

Instantly the spell was broken. Nick wanted to see her body beneath the brilliant blue sky. With the perfection of nature all around them, she would be naked and imperfect.

"No," she whispered. She sat up, pulling her blouse together, tucking her legs beneath her.

The look on Nick's face mixed astonishment and pure male anger. He pushed himself to his feet and glared down at Katie. "No? It's a little late in the game to say no, Kathryn."

"I'm sorry," Katie whispered. She felt lost and desolate, as if Nick were suddenly miles away instead of only a few feet in front of her. She hadn't meant to tease him. For a few moments passion had persuaded her to pretend there was no reason to hold back, then reality had intruded and reminded her there was every reason to hold back. She couldn't spring her imperfections on him. It wouldn't have been fair to Nick, and she knew she couldn't have stood seeing the desire die in his eyes at the sight of her scars.

Nick paced the grass in front of her, his whole body aching with frustration. "You can't push a man that far, then pull away, Katie."

Glancing down at her, Nick cursed himself for losing his temper. Katie was on the verge of tears. The sight tore him apart inside. No matter what she'd done, he didn't want to make her cry. He dropped to his knees in front of her and stroked her hair back from her face. His breath billowed in and out of his lungs. "I know I said I'd wait until you were ready to make love with me, honey. I have waited. I thought now was the right time. I think, Katie, our relationship has reached the point where you can let me in the bedroom door instead of slamming it shut in my face."

Katie stared down at her hands in her lap. She hadn't felt this miserable in a long time. All she could do was wonder who would have been slamming that imaginary door if she had let Nick undress her. How fast would his ardor have cooled if he had gotten to see her scars in the unkind light of day?

"I'm sorry I lost my temper, kitten," he whispered, gathering her against him and kissing her hair. "I just wanted you so much. You're all I think about when I go to bed at night. I lie there awake, wanting you so much I hurt all over."

Katie hugged him back, praying he would understand. "I want you, Nick. I do. But there's something I need to talk to you about first."

"What, sweetheart? If it's about protection, I—"

"No," she said, telling herself that was a logical thing for a man to consider, that she shouldn't let it hurt the way it did. She sniffed back her tears and looked up at Nick. "Let's go down to the house. There's something I have to show you."

A large room had been added onto the back of the old farmhouse. A stone fireplace dominated one end of the room. Thick, taffy-colored carpet stretched across the floor. The furniture looked sturdy and comfortable. The walls were lined with trophies—hundreds of them. There were gold cups, sterling platters, medals hanging on satin ribbons.

Katie led Nick by the hand to a group of photographs that hung above one of the trophy shelves and waited for him to comment. Nick studied the pictures. Each showed a horse and rider catapulting over a massive array of bars, jumps that were high and wide and decorated with potted shrubs and flowers at their bases. They were magnificent photos, capturing the power and beauty of show jumping—and the element of danger as well. It took him a moment to realize the rider in the photographs was Katie. When he did, he turned to her with a stunned expression.

"You asked me if I ever rode in shows," she said. She turned away from him and slowly ran a finger around the edge of a silver champagne bucket that was engraved with the name of a prestigious horse show. "From the time I was five until five years ago riding was my whole life. More than half of these trophies are mine."

"You must have been very good."

"I was good." It was a statement of fact, nothing more. "Riding was all I ever wanted to do. I worked my way up through the different levels of competition. I was twenty-one when I made the move to the grand prix level. That's as high as one can aspire—the best riders in the world, the best horses money can buy, the toughest courses. My goal was to make the Olympic show-jumping team."

Nick expected her to continue the story, but she didn't. She walked to the window and stared out across the pastures toward the misty blue mountains in the distance. She looked as alone as anyone he'd ever seen, wrapped up in some part of her past—a part that somehow had an effect on their relationship.

"What happened?" he asked.

"We were at Lake Placid. It had rained off and on all week, so the footing was a little slick. It wasn't bad really, but you had to be conscious of it, you had to keep that thought in the back of your mind. You couldn't be careless, but I was— just for a second. That's all it took. I misjudged the distance to a big, wide fence, realized it too late, hesitated for a fraction of a second. I pulled back just enough to make my horse lose his foot- ing on the takeoff. He went down in the middle of the jump and landed on top of me."

A wave of sickening fear left Nick shaking all over. It had been difficult to imagine Katie riding the kind of horses that jumped those big fences. To think of a horse that probably weighed around fifteen hundred pounds falling on top of Katie, who didn't top a hundred pounds, made his stom- ach turn over.

"Oh, Katie," he murmured, drawing her into his arms. He needed to hold her, to feel her next to him, and comfort himself with the fact that she had survived. He could have lost her, she could have been killed in the fall, and he never would have had the chance to hold her. The thought made him realize one very important fact: He wasn't falling in love with Katie, he was in love with Katie. He stroked his hand over her hair again and again, as much to soothe himself as Katie. "Thank God you weren't killed."

"I came close," she said. "I fractured three vertebrae in my back, had a compound fracture of my right femur, tore up my knee, crushed my pelvis. The list of body parts I didn't ruin is shorter."

Nick held her for a long time, all the possibilities tumbling in his mind. She could have been killed. She could have been paralyzed. But she hadn't been. She was there in his arms. Still, her fall had had some lasting effect on her life. For some reason she had felt compelled to tell him now, before their relationship progressed any further.

"What does this have to do with us making love, Katie?" he asked softly, pressing his cheek to the top of her head and breathing in the sweet scent of the meadow they'd lain in.

Katie took a deep breath. She couldn't help feeling she was about to cross a line and there would be no turning back. She was stepping over a boundary she had set for herself. Now she understood why some wild animals held in captivity preferred their cages when offered freedom. The cage her accident had placed her in had been a very safe place to be. It had never allowed her to risk rejection.

She stepped back from Nick, determined not to lean on him. She would stand on her own two feet and stay on them no matter what the outcome. There had been too many times she had needed to drag up every ounce of courage and determination she possessed for her to lean on someone else now, no matter how badly she wanted to.

"I have scars," she said slowly, as if each word had to be forced from her mouth. "They're not very pretty."

Nick felt everything fall into place. Suddenly the way Katie had pulled away from him in the pasture made sense. He had wanted to undress her, to be able to look at her, to have nothing between them as they made love. Her scars would have been between them. The scars were the reason Katie had denied them both. They were the reason she had kept her distance from men. They were what had won her the title of Ice Princess.

They were what made a very courageous lady vulnerable.

"That's why you pulled away from me, isn't it?" he asked. She stood before him with her chin up—if quivering a little—obviously prepared for a negative reaction, practically daring him to give her one. "You thought I'd see those scars, and somehow they would change the way I feel about you."

"Why wouldn't they?" she asked quietly, tears shimmering in her eyes. "They changed the way I feel about myself. Why wouldn't they affect you?"

He reached out a hand to touch her cheek. It was as cool and smooth and colorless as porcelain. He wondered how she could be blind to what was in his heart now that it was so obvious to him. "Katie, I love you. No mark on your body could change that."

She forced herself to hold back the feeling of joy that blossomed inside her at his admission. Her confession wasn't over yet. "It's not just the scars, Nick. I didn't leave that accident behind when I got out of the hospital. It will always be with me. There are a lot of things I can't do because of it. I can never ride again. I can never go dancing with you. I can never have children. I want you to know that now, before we go to bed together. I need you to know now, before I fall any more in love with you than I already have."

She was offering him an out. She was telling him their next step would mean more to her than a night of mutual pleasure. But then, he'd already known it would. Katie wouldn't give herself for anything less than love, nor would he have wanted to give her less.

He couldn't tell her dancing wasn't important to him; it had been his life. He couldn't tell her children weren't important to him; he had dreamed of a family. But he could take her in his arms and tell her there had been nothing and no one in his life more important to him than she was.

That was exactly what he did.

SEVEN

THE DRIVE HOME seemed to take forever, yet the time passed too quickly. Katie was nervous, happy, and scared to death all at once. Her emotions were tangled like a cat-tossed ball of yarn. She was so preoccupied, she hardly paid any attention to Nick's driving, which normally kept her on the edge of her seat. She tried to single out individual thoughts from the jumble. Nick was in love with her. Nick wanted her—scars and all.

"I thought your brother was gonna choke when you suggested he ask Maggie to the opening of the Drewes mansion," Nick said, chuckling in remembrance of the look of panic on Ry's face. "Do you think he'll do it?"

"I don't know. You can never tell with Ry. He might ask her, or he might convince himself she'd rather go with a warthog. I think he's interested in Maggie, but he's awfully shy when it comes to women."

Nick shook his head in disbelief. "Shy is not a word I would have associated with your brother, but I wouldn't have guessed he was a wine connoisseur either. I just about dropped my glass when he described that chardonnay as 'capricious with a hint of stateliness.'"

"Ry is full of surprises and secrets."

Not unlike Katie, Nick thought. He guessed most of the people she knew would have been surprised to find out how vulnerable she was beneath her confident, practical exterior. He had sensed the vulnerability in her all along, but he looked more closely than most people did. In telling him about her accident she had let him see a new side of her. Her openness meant almost as much to him as her declaration of love. While she kept everyone else at an emotional arm's length away, she had opened the door for him to see the part of herself she kept hidden from view. Her taking him to meet her brother had been a significant thing too.

Nick glanced at the speedometer and eased his foot off the gas. He was anxious to get to Katie's house, but he certainly didn't want to get a ticket from Peter Ramsey on the way. He shot a quick look at Katie. She was fidgeting. She was going to be nervous. He was as eager to put to rest her fears about her scars as he was to make love to her, but it wasn't going to do any good to talk about it now. Actions definitely were going to speak louder than words. Katie had lived with those physical and emotional scars too long to have them erased by words alone.

"By the way, Ms. Quaid," he said to distract her from working herself into a nervous fit, "do you have a date to the party yet?"

"Why, no, Mr. Leone, I do not," Katie said in her most proper Southern drawl. "I confess, I have been dreaming of going on the arm of the renowned Highwayman. Do you think he might be available?"

"Hmmm...I think something might be arranged.

You do understand he would have to come disguised as a regular guy, don't you?"

"Naturally." Since Katie had discovered Nick's secret profession, it had become something of a joke between them. It put her at ease to tease him about it now when she was so nervous. "He does realize he will have to keep his clothes on, doesn't he?"

"Clothes? You expect him to wear clothes?"

"Everything except his mask."

"How about the mask and nothing else?" He chuckled at the look Katie gave him. She had the greatest repertoire of stern expressions. "Ah, well, maybe later on in the evening. He probably could be persuaded to wear a tux to begin with."

The moment of truth was at hand, Katie thought as Nick parked at the curb in front of her house, got out, and went around to help her out of the low-sitting car. Watch pushed his way out of the backseat, bounded over the gate and into the yard. Katie's mind was so crowded with thoughts of how the rest of the evening was going to go, she was only dimly aware of Nick holding her hand as they strolled up the sidewalk. At the door he pressed a soft kiss to her mouth and left the rest up to her.

She swallowed hard. "Um ... would you like to come in?"

"I'd like that very much," he said with a gentle smile.

Katie's heart was hammering in her chest like some sort of demented gong. The vibrations of it shimmied through her until she thought her teeth were going to begin chattering. Did she really have to go along with the whole ritual of offering Nick a drink, then sitting on the sofa, sweating it out until he made a move? They both knew how they wanted the evening to end. What was the point in waiting?

She turned as he stepped into the living room, took a deep breath, and blurted out, "I'd really like for you to spend the night."

Nick's heart went out to her at the horrified look on her face. She pressed her hands to her cheeks. "Oh, rats, I shouldn't have said that!"

"Why not?" he asked, easing his arms around her. "It was what I wanted to hear."

"I mean, I should have said it better— differently—oh, blast," she muttered, dropping her forehead against his chest. "I'm no good at this, Nick. I've never seduced a man in my life."

"I don't need to be seduced, kitten." He ran a hand down her back over the silky curtain of her hair. "Are you nervous?"

"What kind of a damn fool question is that?" she asked, scowling at him. "Of course I'm nervous."

"It's okay, you know, sweetheart. It's okay to be a little nervous."

"I'm darn near choking on it. Is that okay?"

He couldn't help chuckling at her panic. She was so cute when she got rattled. Her eyebrows dropped down in annoyance, and her voice turned all smoky. He wondered what it would sound like in the afterglow of passion.

Katie wanted to belt him for looking so amused. There was a threat of impending fury in her voice when she spoke. "Don't you dare laugh at me."

Nick shook his head, sobering. "I'm not laughing at you, sweetheart. I just know there's no reason for you to be so nervous. Making love with you is going to be a beautiful experience."

Automatically she spread a hand across her stomach. "Poor choice of words, I think."

"No." He drew her hand away from her stomach, lifting it to place a kiss in her palm. "I think it was the perfect word. I think the physical expression of feelings between two people who love each other can be nothing short of beautiful."

Katie looked up into Nick's warm, sincere eyes, and felt calmer. Nick didn't say things he didn't mean, and when he looked at her so intensely, it was difficult for her to feel anything less than absolute trust. He was the man she had chosen. Trust was one of the reasons. He had been so patient with her, so sweet, so considerate of her feelings. She tried to concentrate on that thought as she took Nick's hand and led him to her bedroom.

Moonlight filtered in through the lace curtains—cool, colorless light that cut across the bed at an angle. It was enough light to satisfy Katie, but still she went to the stand beside her bed and turned on the little china lamp with the ruffled shade. She wasn't going to leave any room for doubt, nor was she going to be a coward.

She turned to Nick and waited.

He lifted his hands to the first button on her

blouse, the uncertainty in her eyes tugging at his heartstrings. She looked as if she were about to face a firing squad. "Kitten, I can guarantee you, I won't find anything under these clothes that won't make me the happiest guy around," he murmured in his most seductive tone of voice. "Except . . . you don't have any tattoos, do you? I can handle scars, but tattoos . . ." He shook his head disapprovingly. "I draw the line at tattoos."

A bright smile lifted her lips. It was just like Nick to try to put her at ease, she thought. She shook her head. "No tattoos."

"Me either." He grinned, then said seriously, "I will warn you, my belly button is slightly off center and I have a mole on my stomach."

"I know what you look like," Katie said, unbuttoning his shirt with fingers that suddenly seemed too clumsy to accomplish the simple task. She laughed at her own ineptitude. "Half the female population of the East Coast knows." She teased him with a skeptical look as her hands stilled. "You're not going to charge me for looking, are you?"

"Smart aleck." He shrugged his shirt off and dropped it to the floor. Katie backed up as he advanced on her, her face alight with mischief and nervous anticipation. When she bumped into the nightstand, she made a move to dart around Nick, but he caught her in his arms and tickled her mercilessly.

"Oh—don't—stop!" she said between gasps, squirming against him. "Nick, please!"

"Remember those lines later on," he suggested. Tickles turned to caresses as his mouth lowered to hers. He kissed her long and leisurely, until her mouth turned hot and soft beneath his and he felt her melt against him. Her blouse joined his shirt on the floor, then her skirt floated down to pool on the rug.

Nick's hands molded around every inch of her he could reach as he kissed her. His fingertips traced every delicate curve and line. She was so dainty it took his breath away and made his hands tremble. Lowering one knee to the bed, he trailed kisses down her throat to her breasts, which were small but somehow more feminine because of it. They were creamy with a tracery of blue veins just beneath the surface and coral-colored tips that begged his mouth's attention.

Katie's breath left her on a sigh. She braced her

hands on Nick's broad shoulders and leaned into the heat of his mouth. It was everything she could do not to hold him there when she felt his fingertips catch in the waistband of her panties, but she forced herself to be still. His kisses trailed lower still as he sank down on the bed and dragged away the final barrier of her clothing.

There were scars, all right, Nick thought as he ran a hand across her belly. And there was nothing beautiful about them. But they did nothing to change the way he wanted Katie. For a split second he relived the fear he'd felt when she had told him about the accident that had given her these scars, then he relived his first realization of being in love with her. The feeling flowed through him even stronger now than it had then.

Katie had gone utterly still as Nick uncovered her. She waited and prayed and held her breath until her lungs burned, while he looked at her without saying a word. Her imagination ran wild with what-if questions. What if the scars were worse than he had anticipated? Katie always had told herself they looked worse to her than they really were, but what if she'd been wrong? Nick had promised her they wouldn't matter to him.

What if he realized now he'd made a promise he couldn't keep?

When he drew her nearer and began to press kisses to the flaws that marred her skin, tears of relief flooded Katie's eyes. As weakness washed over her, her knees lost their strength, but Nick held her, his arms around her legs. He went on kissing her, tracing his lips over each line. When he finished, he rose and turned back the covers of the bed, lifted Katie, and placed her on the cool cotton sheets.

She watched him undress, in awe of his male beauty. She had seen the power and athletic artistry of his body as he had danced. Everything he did he did with an unconscious grace—even getting into bed. He settled beside her with shining eyes and a sweet smile.

"So, here we are," he said.

"Here we are," she repeated absently, all caught up in the contrast of his dark skin against the snow-white sheets. Her gaze traveled the length of him as he lay stretched out on his side. She had seen most of his body before as he'd whirled beneath the hot lights of the stage at Hepplewhite's.

The parts that were new to her were no less beautiful, no less male than the rest of him.

Nick ran his hand down her side, over the curve of her slender hip. "You're so tiny," he murmured. He was going to have to hold his passion in check, even though he wanted her more than he'd ever wanted any woman.

"You're not," Katie said, dragging her gaze upward and fixing it on the width of his muscular chest. He seemed bigger than ever, in her bed, dwarfing her in every way.

"Don't worry," said Nick, dropping a soft kiss to her lips. "I'll be so gentle with you, kitten. I wouldn't hurt you for the world. I love you."

"I love you," she echoed.

"Then come here and touch me."

He pulled her a little closer, then took her hand on a guided tour of his body. The first stop was his chest. Her fingers brushed over the mat of black curls, teased the brown nipples until they were pebble hard. His response to her touch brought about a mirror reaction in Katie's body. Her breasts tingled. He drew her hand down across the hard, flat plane of his belly, following the line of hair that skipped around his navel, down to the hard, proud shaft of his manhood. He closed her hand around him, groaning as she stroked him hesitantly. She groaned in return at the ache deep in her belly.

Nick tipped her face up and kissed her. His hand set off on an exploration of her body, stroking, teasing, marveling at her softness. He wanted her so badly, he felt nearly frantic, but he clung to his control. Everything had to be perfect for her this first time. It seemed as if it were the most important task he'd ever had entrusted to him—to make love to Katie with complete tenderness, to make her feel beautiful and feminine and cherished, to show her nothing mattered more to him than the way he felt about her.

He wouldn't rush her, but he couldn't stand what she was doing to him for much longer. He rolled Katie onto her back and made his way down her body, kissing and tasting. She squirmed beneath him, giggling as his teeth tickled her ribs, gasping as his tongue dipped into her navel. He burned a path down one silky leg and up the other.

Finally he eased a pillow beneath her hips and knelt between her parted thighs. He stroked her with one hand and guided himself into her with the other, groaning as her velvet warmth closed tightly around him.

Katie bit her lip and took all of him, stunned at the emotions that belonging to him evoked. There was love, achingly sweet and as special as she had always imagined it should be. There was a soaring joy entwined with a strong sense of being set free. Nick was setting her free from the bondage of her scars. If he never gave her anything more, it would be enough. She would love him for it always, for making her feel beautiful and cherished and whole.

She reached out to him, wanting no distance between them. She wanted her arms around him, their hearts pressed together. She wanted to touch him, to feel the flex and strain of his muscles as he moved on top of her and inside her.

"Kiss me," she whispered as he lowered himself, taking his weight on his arms. His mouth moved across hers in a caress as sensuous as the caress of his body against hers.

Their loving was slow and tender; they smiled and whispered their love. Gazes locked and legs tangled, they moved together, giving and taking until one could no longer be distinguished from the other. Need and pleasure built together, feeding on each other, growing to a climax that shook them both with its intensity.

Afterward Katie snuggled against Nick's side, with her head pressed to his shoulder, her hand over his heart. She felt exhausted, utterly content, irrevocably changed in a way she couldn't explain.

"Do I get to say I told you so?" Nick asked, his voice low and gravelly as if he hadn't the energy left to speak in his normal tone.

Katie raised up on one elbow and smiled down at him. "I don't think that's necessary. Nick, I had no idea it would be so..." Words failed her, and her voice trailed off as she gave up her attempt to explain.

He reached up and brushed back her bangs and murmured, "Me either." He couldn't begin to tell her how special he'd felt holding her and loving her, feeling her body respond to his and knowing he was the only man who had ever experienced such joy with her. Making love was nothing new to Nick, but what he had just shared with Katie was entirely new. He couldn't begin to articulate his feelings, but he could see from the expression in her eyes, he didn't need to. Katie understood.

She was all peaches and cream in the soft lamp-light. He lifted a hand to cup her breast and smiled at her intake of breath. "Are you sure you're not Miss Nude Universe? You look a lot like her."

"I think you need your glasses, Leone," she said dryly.

"Naw, forget them," he said. "They'd only be steaming up right about now."

Tracing a finger along the clear-cut edges of his lips, she said, "You have the sexiest mouth." She leaned down and kissed him lightly. His right ear captured her attention next. "Your ears are nice too. I noticed them the first time we met."

"Did you?"

She nodded, pushing a lock of dark hair back behind her own ear. "I thought you were very at-tractive, and it made me mad."

"Why would that make you mad?"

"Because I didn't want to be attracted to you," she said, deciding to be honest with him. There didn't seem to be any point in holding back now. "Because I was sure you wouldn't be attracted to me. Because I thought I could never have more out of life than I already had."

"And now?"

"And now," she said with a wry smile, "I'm willing to admit I was wrong. But don't spread that news around. It would ruin my reputation for being stubborn."

Nick's brows rose in mock surprise. "You? Stubborn?"

"Don't get smart with me, Yankee." She laughed and hugged him with more strength than she thought she had left, and then raised up to give him a challenging look. "Remember the way you made me feel a little while ago? I dare you to make me feel that way again."

His crooked grin flashed brilliantly across his dark face. "You're on, lady."

Katie woke up alone. Soft yellow sunlight and a fresh breeze spilled in through her bedroom window. From the direction of her kitchen came the muted clatter of pots and pans.

So last night hadn't been a dream after all, she thought. Nick really had spent the night schooling her in the fine art of lovemaking. She stretched and groaned as her body protested at the movement, muscles she never had imagined having aching. Nick had been exquisitely careful with her, never letting her take his weight, never putting too much pressure on her back, but still she was stiff and sore.

She eased herself to a sitting position and rubbed her eyes. Ordinarily she bounced out of bed in the morning, disgustingly chipper and ready to take on the day. Today she wanted nothing more than to sink back on the mattress and laze the day away with Nick beside her. She had to force herself out of bed.

The reflection of her naked body in the cheval glass caught her attention. She turned carefully and faced the mirror. Her long dark hair tumbled wildly all around her. She was going to have a devil of a time getting a comb through it this morning, but she didn't really care. Nick had wanted it loose. He loved the feel of it against his skin, loved to bury his hands in it.

Katie always had thought there wasn't much to her body. She wasn't shapely, didn't have the kind of figure that turned male heads. This morning she felt rounder somehow, more feminine than she had ever felt in her life, a hundred times more feminine than she had felt since her hysterectomy. And when she looked at the reflection of the scars that crisscrossed her stomach, they didn't seem quite as ugly as they had the day before.

Maybe in time they wouldn't seem very important at all. She wanted to think so as the beautiful sounds and scents of late spring poured through her window. Optimism was an abundant commodity on such a day, especially after a night spent in Nick's arms.

Throwing on a blue silk robe, Katie padded barefoot to the kitchen. Nick was busy at the counter arranging bowls and utensils. He was barefoot, too, wearing nothing but his jeans. It seemed impossible for a man to look so sexy in a pair of worn denims, but he did. There was something about the way his back tapered from broad shoulders to his narrow waist and gorgeous backside that made her breath stick in her lungs. Her heart thudded in her chest as memories of the night came back to her. There wasn't an inch of his body she hadn't explored. He knew hers just as well.

"Good morning," she said softly, suddenly feeling shy. She'd never had a lover before. How was a person supposed to act the morning after?

He'd been right, Nick thought as he glanced over his shoulder at her. Her voice was low and husky in the morning. The two words she'd spoken had him wanting to tumble her back into bed, but he knew that wasn't going to be possible. He had known better than to make love to her so long into the night when she was inexperienced, but Katie had been a very willing and persuasive partner. He could see by her careful movements, she was paying the price this morning.

"Hi, kitten," he murmured, turning completely around to take her in his arms. She snuggled against him, pressing her cheek to his warm, solid chest. "How are you feeling this morning? Any regrets?"

She looked up at him, her eyes clear and full of love. "No. Do you have any?"

He nodded. Her heart skipped. "I regret to inform you your kitchen is a wasteland. You have no food. No wonder you're so little."

"I have food," she said in her own defense. "You must not have looked in the freezer."

"I looked in the freezer." He frowned. "My mama would weep if she knew you were eating boil-in-the-bag cacciatore."

"Well, I don't eat it for breakfast. I'm sure there are some toaster waffles in there."

"Yeah. They're right next to the imitation fruit and cardboard turnovers." Nick shook his head in reproach and turned back to the counter as Katie moved to stand by the sink. "I managed to scrape together the makings of French toast. You had half a loaf of unbearably stale bread. I can't think of anything better to do with it. I suppose I'll be lucky if there aren't baby chickens in these eggs. Fresh is too much to hope for."

"Fussy," Katie muttered. She glanced at the clock on the stove and winced. "Oh, Nick, I'm afraid I don't have time for breakfast. I'm going to be late for work as it is."

He caught her by the arm as she headed back toward the bedroom. "You've got all the time in the world. I called Maggie and told her you'd be late."

"You what?" Katie asked, incredulous. "Nick, how could you?"

He laughed. "It wasn't news to her. Myrtle

Kelly already had informed her that my car was parked outside your house all night."

Katie covered her face with her hands and shook her head. Small towns! Every store clerk and gas station attendant in Briarwood would know before noon that the mysterious Nick Leone had managed to thaw the town's ice princess.

Nick went still as he watched her blush. "Do you mind having people know about us?" he asked quietly. He pulled her hands down and held them in his, feeling uncertain. Katie had a position in the community. Being seen in public with him was one thing. Having everyone know they were lovers was something else. "Do you mind having the gossips speculating about you and the nefarious guy from Jersey?"

Katie gave him one of her no-nonsense looks. "Oh, pooh, let them think what they want. My friends are the only people I care about when it comes to my reputation. They may not know exactly who you are, but they like you anyway. As for the rest of the town, they can gossip to their hearts' content. I'm embarrassed, though, that you would just call someone up and tell them I'm too exhausted from making love with you to come in to work."

That was Katie, he thought, prim and proper. There certainly hadn't been anything prim or proper about her in bed, and Nick was the only one who knew. The thought brought him immense satisfaction.

"I love you," he said with an exuberant grin. Without giving her any warning at all, he swung Katie up into his arms and strode toward the bedroom. Instead of depositing her on the bed, he turned right and nudged the bathroom door open with his toe.

"Just what are you planning, Mr. Leone?" Katie asked in a haughty tone.

"You've heard of breakfast in bed. This is breakfast in bath."

The room was every bit as large as Katie's bedroom, but it was partitioned into two sections, and an enormous white bathtub with polished brass faucets and ball and claw feet stood in the center of the first. Potted ferns were grouped around it on the gleaming wood floor. A brass towel rack stood nearby.

Nick lowered Katie to a vanity chair and

started the water running in the tub. He selected a bottle of bubble bath from the small glass-topped table beside the tub and poured in enough for three baths. Katie suppressed the urge to giggle at the serious look on his face as he arranged the lush peach towels on the rack. Then he came to her, stood her up, and slid her robe off her shoulders, his gaze roaming hungrily over her body as the blue silk slipped to the floor. He swept her up into his arms, holding her high against his chest so he could nuzzle her breasts as he carried her to the tub.

The water was hot and heavenly and silky from too much bubble bath. Katie sank down into it with a grateful sigh that turned to a sputter as the bubbles threatened to engulf her. She brushed them away from her face and tilted a smile up at Nick, who was looking very pleased with himself.

"Did I hear you mention something about breakfast?" she asked sweetly.

He knelt down beside the tub and ran a finger coated with tiny bubbles down her nose. "Yeah, but now that I see you in this tub I think I've changed my mind about French toast. I'm hungrier for you."

He tried to kiss her and got a mouthful of bubbles for his trouble. Katie laughed. "You'd better wait until the suds die down, Romeo."

"How long will that take?"

"About as long as it takes to make and eat French toast."

While Nick was in the kitchen, Katie put her hair up with pins she kept on the table next to the tub. She leaned back in the steaming water and closed her eyes as the stiffness seeped out of her muscles and joints. It was nice to feel lazy and decadent for a change. It would be easy to get used to having Nick pamper her.

Too easy, a little voice deep inside her warned.

Katie ignored it. Hadn't she decided practically from the start to take one day at a time with Nick and let the chips fall where they might? So far things were working out. There was no sense worrying about some day in the future. Nick loved her. He made her feel special, made her forget about her scars. She loved him.

"Breakfast is now being served in the bathtub," Nick announced. The tray he carried in bore a single plate piled with French toast dripping in maple syrup, two glasses of orange juice, and a bud vase with flowers Katie recognized from her garden. He dragged the little vanity chair up next to the tub and sat down, balancing the tray on his legs.

"This is heavenly," Katie said with a groan of appreciation after Nick had presented her with the first bite. "I taste apples."

"I found a couple that hadn't petrified in the back of the refrigerator."

"And I taste spices."

He shrugged. "A little cinnamon, a little nutmeg."

"This beats the heck out of a toaster waffle."

"I should hope so."

Nick ate, but mostly he watched Katie. She was glowing, smiling at the least provocation. There was rosy color in her cheeks. Making love all night agreed with her. He was glad, because he planned to make a habit of it.

"Shouldn't you be at the restaurant?" she asked, brushing back a strand of hair that had escaped her haphazard topknot. "I thought today was the day they were putting in the much ballyhooed curb and gutter."

"It is, but not until later on. We have plenty of time to get there."

"We?" Katie arched a brow at him.

Nick bit his lip and gave her his most hopeful look. "I was hoping you might be persuaded to help me sort through the plates and utensils I bought at that auction in Richmond last week."

"Is that what this breakfast in the bath business is all about?" Katie asked with amusement showing plainly through the stern expression she was trying to maintain.

"No, I—"

"It's going to take more than a little French toast, Mr. Leone."

"Really? What did you have in mind?" he asked, setting the tray on the floor and leaning over the tub. He dabbed at the corner of Katie's mouth with a napkin. "You have syrup on you."

"I can think of a more imaginative way to get it off," she said suggestively.

A wicked grin spread across his face. He leaned toward her, his tongue working at the dot of syrup, then probing the corner of Katie's mouth. She let her hands wander over his chest as they kissed, tracing wet patterns over his bare skin down to the waistband of his jeans. One finger dipped inside the denim to tickle him.

Nick cleared his throat, lifting his mouth from hers just enough to speak. "Katie, what are you doing?"

"Seducing you. Am I doing it right?"

Doing it right? he wondered. If she got any better at it, he was going to be in a lot of trouble. "We shouldn't make love again." Even as he said the words he was hoping she would disagree with him.

"Shouldn't we?" She looked so innocent—too innocent to be believed, he told himself. "Okay, but would you give me another kiss?"

He obliged her without hesitation. The heat was instantaneous, burning away any good intentions he'd had. She tasted too sweet, was too willing. Without taking his mouth from hers, Nick shucked his pants. He was sliding down into the tub behind Katie before she knew what was happening.

"Nick! What are you doing?" She squealed as water sloshed and lapped at the rim of the tub. She had enjoyed teasing him a little, but she had thought he would wait until she'd gotten out of the tub to further their amorous activities.

"It's part of the breakfast-in-the-tub special," he said, sliding his arms around her as his long legs stretched out on either side of her. His hands found her soap-slick breasts and began massaging them. He nipped at her earlobe. "The cook gets to have his way with you after the main course."

"Is that an old Italian custom?" she asked, gasping as he lifted her, then closing her eyes and sighing as he eased her down on him. She leaned back into him, loving the feel of having him deep inside her.

"No." He grazed her shoulder with his teeth. "It's a new Nick and Katie custom."

Breathlessly she said, "There's nothing quite as exciting as a new custom."

"Hear, hear."

EIGHT

AS SPRING WARMED into summer, Katie found her days pleasantly filled to capacity. She and Maggie had more than enough business to keep them busy. What spare time she had was devoted to helping Nick around the restaurant or helping out at the Drewes mansion, where the renovation was nearing completion. Evenings were spent with Nick, when he wasn't working at Hepplewhite's.

Katie was surprised and pleased to find they had many common interests. Even though he had spent his entire life in cities that were fast paced and exciting, Nick seemed to enjoy quieter pursuits. He liked movies—especially murder mysteries spiced with romance—and popcorn with no butter but lots of salt. He liked relaxing with a good book, a glass of wine, and soft music in the background. He liked lying in bed with Katie in his arms, sharing quiet talk and gentle lovemaking.

She found herself more and more in love with Nick. It was a fascinating experience, one she never had had or expected to have. The world seemed a bright and wonderful place. Her senses seemed more acute—colors were more vibrant, sounds clearer, tastes more delightful. She never had really believed love could change a person's perceptions so, but she believed it now. She had to laugh at herself for behaving as if she were a starstruck girl. It was very unlike her, but she reveled in every minute of it.

There were moments when she caught herself thinking it was too good to be true. Every so often questions about the future would creep into her mind. Where was her romance with Nick headed? She had stepped off the cautious path she had guided her life along for the last few years. Where was she now—on the road to happiness or heart-ache?

How long would it take before Nick realized she was holding him back from having everything he wanted? While he seemed content with the quiet evenings they were spending together, how long would it be before he grew restless and began longing for a woman who could be as active as he was capable of being, a woman he could go dancing with, a woman he could wrestle with in bed instead of one he had to be careful with? How long would it be before he would want a woman he could plan a family with?

More often than not Katie pushed the questions away without even attempting to answer them. It made her furious to have doubts infringe on her happiness with Nick. She deserved to have this time with him. She deserved to have him love her. And she refused to let black thoughts about the future ruin her mood.

Katie felt herself blossom as her friendship with Nick deepened and strengthened with their love. She felt relaxed and happy with him. They talked about everything from Broadway musicals to the beauty of the Blue Ridge Mountains. And they teased each other constantly about their respective accents and regional differences.

Many evenings they took slow, relaxing walks, admiring people's gardens, enjoying small talk and the warm weather. They often stopped to chat with people who were out tending their lawns or sitting on their porches. He had an insatiable curiosity about his new neighbors.

"I like to talk to everybody I meet here just so I can listen to their accent," Nick commented as they strolled one evening. On his right side he held Watch's leash. His left hand held Katie's, but he dropped it often so he could express himself more fully.

"Accent?" Katie arched a brow. "Isn't that exactly what a Yankee would say. Does it ever occur to Northerners that y'all are the ones with the accent?"

"Yawl, yawl," Nick said in an exaggerated drawl. He shot Katie a teasing grin. "What's *yawl*?"

Katie gave him a saccharine smile. "It's a two-masted sailing vessel, but why would you ask? Oh, forgive me, I forgot, there isn't anything you people from New Jersey don't find fascinating to talk about. It's no wonder y'all talk so fast; you never run out of things to say."

"Are you saying I talk too much?" he questioned indignantly, stopping on the sidewalk and turning to face Katie with a fierce expression that was as phony as a three-dollar bill. He held one hand on his hip and gestured with the other. "Is that what you're saying to me—that I talk too much?"

Grabbing Nick's hands, Katie raised up on tiptoe. Holding his hands still was almost as effective in getting him to stop talking as taping his mouth shut. "Shut up and kiss me, Yankee," she said in a smoky tone of voice that drove Nick wild.

He pressed his lips to hers for a quick kiss that turned into a leisurely kiss, as hot and slow as a Southern summer night. She brushed against him, her fingers playing with his hair where it curled against the back of his neck as his tongue curled around hers. Their bodies lingered against each other as their lips broke contact reluctantly.

Katie's voice was a low, seductive purr when she spoke. "By chance, we happen to be right outside my house. Shall we go in and discuss our regional dissimilarities further?"

"I think I'd rather discuss our anatomical dis-similarities, if it's all the same to you."

"It's not all the same," she pointed out with a saucy grin, more than a little aroused by the smol-dering fires in his dark eyes. "That's what makes it fun."

With a devilish chuckle, he started to turn toward the house but stopped. Standing stock-still on the sidewalk no more than three feet from Watch were two little girls. The older was perhaps five. She wore a gingham sundress and held the hand of a chubby toddler dressed in a sunsuit. Both had bright red hair, and blue eyes that were opened wide as they stared at the panting wolf-hound.

They were adorable, Nick thought as he knelt down, but then, he was a sucker for little girls. If he ever had daughters of his own, they were going to get away with murder. He stroked the dog ab-sently and smiled at the little girls. "Hi there. Are you ladies lost?"

The older girl shook her head. She pointed to the house next door to Katie's. "Our grandma lives there. That sure is a big dog."

"He's big all right," Nick said. As if on cue,

Watch turned and licked his cheek. "But he's real friendly."

The baby's face split into a cherubic grin. She giggled and pointed at the dog. "Puppy."

Nick laughed. They were priceless. The older one had her hair up in an off-center ponytail and carried a big green purse she undoubtedly had borrowed from her grandmother. The little one wore yellow rabbit barrettes in her fine hair and pink Popsicle stains on her face.

"He's a nice puppy. Would you like to pet him?" he asked. As they nodded hesitantly, Nick glanced over his shoulder to get Katie's permission. He had expected to see her smiling, as delighted by the two urchins as he was. What he saw was a pale face and a pair of gray eyes so filled with despair, it was like taking a punch in the gut to see them. "Katie?" he asked gently, "is it okay for them to pet the dog?"

Willing her lips to turn up in a smile, Katie choked down the lump in her throat and tried to sound normal. "Of course. Watch loves children."

And so did Nick. He looked so natural with the little girls, so at ease. She envied him. It was a trait she had never possessed, because she had never spent any time around small children. It was a trait she would never cultivate now, because to give herself that freely to other people's children was like tearing out bits of her heart and giving them away. Obviously it wasn't the same for Nick. What a wonderful father he would make someday—someday, for some other woman's children, she thought.

It wasn't difficult for Katie to hold her tears out of sight behind her eyes. She had done it many times before. The mask of polite interest slipped into place automatically, if a little late.

She knelt down beside Nick and helped him show the little girls all of Watch's favorite places to get scratched. Then she excused herself and went to the house, hoping Nick would linger outside long enough for her to push her feelings into the little box she usually kept them locked in deep inside her. If she was very, very lucky, he wouldn't ask any questions.

She was in the kitchen pouring lemonade from a sweating pitcher into iced glasses when he came in. She heard the door close, heard his footsteps on the heart-pine floor of the living room. He stopped at the entrance to the kitchen. She could feel his gaze on her.

"Is it really so difficult for you?" he asked.

The urge to cry crashed into her like a tidal wave. Katie swore under her breath. She never dissolved into tears in front of people—never. The problem was, the scene on the sidewalk had taken her by surprise. Old feelings of hurt had surged to the surface before she'd had a chance to stop them. Now Nick was offering her an outlet for those feelings, but one of her greatest fears had been that once she started to let those feelings out, they would never stop, they would pour out in a flood tide and drown her.

Very deliberately she raised her glass to her lips and took a sip of the cold drink, letting it wash down her hot, dry throat. When she spoke she sounded in control. "Sometimes."

He didn't understand. He was trying, but Katie could see he didn't understand. She could have explained it to him in the concise, clinical way of a psychologist. She could have told him that the ideal process for the successful resolution of feelings toward infertility were not unlike the stages toward acceptance of death. She could have explained that while most of the time she felt as if she had completely accepted her fate, she sometimes fell back into the anger stage because she was a goal-oriented person who was being denied a life goal. She could have explained that she often didn't feel entitled to her sense of loss because she had willingly chosen to participate in a dangerous sport and felt she had to accept the consequences. She could have explained, but she didn't want to.

How could she expect him to understand the kind of loss she had suffered? How could she possibly make him understand the hollow feeling she got knowing she would never experience pregnancy, would never know what it was to feel her child grow inside her, to give it life, to nurse it at her breast. How could he feel any of her emotions? He was a man. He couldn't feel the loss of a privilege that had never been his.

Nick hated it when she shut him out. He could feel her going inside her emotional isolation booth and vowed to stick his foot in the door before she could close it.

"Katie," he said, reaching out to her, "talk to

me. Help me understand what you're feeling. Don't shut me out."

She moved to look out the window above the sink, effectively dodging contact with him, but she didn't voice an objection when he stepped behind her and corralled her against the counter with an arm on either side of her. She sighed and resigned herself to giving him as brief an explanation as he would accept.

"After my mother left us, I used to lie awake nights thinking about the children I would have when I grew up, and what a wonderful mother I'd be. It will never happen to me, Nick. It hurts."

The intensity of the hurt had taken her by surprise. It always stung a little to encounter children—she expected it. But it had been years since the pain had been as sharp as when she'd looked down at Nick and those two darling little redheads. Weeks ago she had seen him with Zoe's little daughter in his arms. What she'd felt then had been nothing in comparison. The difference, she realized, was that she hadn't been in love with him then.

It hurt him too. It cut at Nick's heart to see Katie in pain. He knew how full of love she was.

She could be cool and aloof, but he knew that behind her shield was a woman who was perhaps too sensitive, too easily hurt. Glimpses of the vulnerable side of Katie never failed to bring out his protective instincts, never failed to make him love her more. He wrapped his arms around her and drew her back against his body.

"It's not an all or nothing proposition," he said softly, following her gaze as she stared out the window. Watch rolled on his back in the grass with an enormous rawhide bone in his mouth. "Adoption is a perfectly good alternative."

"Not for me."

"Why not?"

Why not? Because she didn't want to be a single parent, and what man was going to want someone else's children when he was perfectly capable of fathering his own? Why not? Because what she knew of the process seemed so cold, analytical, and businesslike. It reminded her too much of people coming to the farm to buy foals— weeding through the crop, looking for what characteristics were important to them. The whole procedure made her question her own reasons for wanting to become a parent in the first place.

If he wanted to hear deeper reasons, they were there as well. But Katie didn't offer them to him. In love with him or not, she was too used to keeping her own counsel to open up her innermost self for examination by Nick.

She said simply, "It just isn't."

"That's not a reason, Katie, that's stubbornness. Lots of people adopt kids. It's an option to give you what you want—why won't you look at it?"

Anger that had been simmering just under the surface bubbled up. She turned in his arms and tried to push him away. She didn't succeed, but he took the hint and stepped back. "I've had five years to look at it," she said, glaring up at him. "I've lain awake nights looking at it. How long have you spent looking at it, five minutes?"

The last thing he'd meant to do was add to her hurt, yet he'd done so with his careless advice. The evidence of his mistake shimmered in her eyes and trembled on her wide, soft mouth. He could have kicked himself. Hitching his hands to his hips he sighed in defeat. "I'm sorry. I shouldn't have—"

"No, you shouldn't have," she said. Abandoning her drink on the counter she walked stiffly past Nick to the bathroom and shut herself inside.

She half expected him to be gone when she came back out nearly half an hour later. She had needed the time by herself to regain control, to raise her defensive shield of cool composure, to put all her feelings back into their compartments where they usually stayed. Maybe she had wanted Nick to take some time to think too. Maybe if he thought about the situation, he would opt out now.

She wouldn't blame Nick. It wasn't his fault she couldn't give him a family. It didn't do any good to rail against fate either. She knew; she'd already wasted too much time doing that. But it was hard not to curse her fate. After everything that had happened, didn't she deserve some compensation? She loved Nick—deeply, selfishly, possessively. The last thing she wanted was to let him go.

Methodically she went through her bedtime ritual of washing her face, brushing her teeth, combing out and braiding her waist-length hair. Physically and emotionally drained she undressed, dropping her clothes into the white wicker hamper.

She slipped into the robe she kept on a hook beside the door, belting it snugly.

Taking a deep breath to clam herself, Katie sank down onto the vanity chair and leaned her elbows on her knees. She was overreacting. The subject of children had blindsided her, and she automatically had turned defensive. Now she calmly made a mental list of her attributes, of the positive things she could bring to a relationship. She reviewed the bright side of her life—good friends, a business she had built and was extremely proud of.

She couldn't have children and had decided against adoption after a great deal of soul-searching. It wasn't the end of the world. A fulfilling, meaningful life was not based on one's ability to reproduce. She would have to sit down with Nick and explain her feelings to him like the cool-headed, responsible adult she normally was. All she had to do now was hope he hadn't left after deciding she was a raving lunatic.

Nick wasn't gone.

Katie stepped from the bathroom to find her bedroom aglow with candlelight—a soft, honey-gold light that warmed the peach-colored walls to a rich melon hue. The shades had been drawn, the bedclothes turned down invitingly. The radio on the table beside her bed murmured a slow, romantic song. There was a single peach rose lying on her pillow. And there was Nick with his sincere dark gaze on her and his arms open wide.

Feeling as if she had just received a reprieve, Katie walked into his embrace and fell even more deeply in love with him. Her lips trailed across his chest as her arms went around him, and tears of relief tried to force their way out from behind the barrier of her tightly closed lids.

"I'm sorry," she whispered, not quite certain what she was apologizing for—for flying off the handle, for leaving him alone, for not being able to have his children?

Nick's hand slid over her hair as he held her close. "Shh, it's all right, kitten. I'm sorry too. We'll work it out."

We'll work it out. Katie had a feeling the statement meant something different to each of them. To her it meant she would be able to convince Nick she had made the only decision she could. To Nick it probably meant he thought he would be able to convince her to choose the alternative open to her.

For the moment Katie couldn't let their differences of opinion matter. All that mattered was being in Nick's arms and letting love and desire control her actions and responses. He was hers to hold, to touch, to tease. She never wanted to let him go.

That one thought filled her mind as Nick's hands parted her robe and claimed her aching breasts. It filled her head as he laid her down on the sheets and filled with his hardness the aching emptiness between her thighs.

He was hers, and she never wanted to let him go.

NINE

"WHAT IS THIS thing?" Maggie asked, poking at the stainless-steel box that sat in the middle of Nick's new kitchen. Thunder rumbled overhead. "It looks dangerous."

Nick paused in his task of adjusting the shelves in the reach-in refrigerator to glance over his shoulder. "That's a plate elevator." He slid the refrigerator door shut and approached his latest kitchen toy to demonstrate. "The plates go in here, see? It's spring-loaded, so every time a waitress takes a plate off, a new one pops up to the top."

"I had no idea there was so much machinery

involved in running a restaurant," she said, her curious gaze roaming around the room.

Nick proudly looked around. He had worked like a demon to get his kitchen in shape. Now freshly painted yellow walls made a cheery background for the equipment he'd purchased. There was the brand-new stove he had spent too much money on. The ice maker, plate elevator, and reach-in refrigerator had all been bought used to get his budget back in line. The center of the room was dominated by a long, high worktable with a butcher block at one end and a sink at the other. Pots of various sizes hung from an iron rack overhead.

"Maggie," Katie called, stepping in from the dining room. "I thought you were going to help me decide on the arrangement of these things for the walls."

"I am." She puffed up her red hair and batted her lashes at Nick. "Just as soon as I steal your beau away from you, Kathryn."

"If you're looking for a date to the big party at the Drewes mansion, he's already spoken for," Katie said, moving to the counter where Nick had been sorting through his hundreds of recipe cards.

She fussed unnecessarily with the stacks, trying to appear nonchalant. "Has anyone asked you yet?"

"Carter Hill," Maggie replied with no enthusiasm. Frowning, she stared at the rain that poured down on the other side of the kitchen screen door.

Katie and Nick exchanged a nervous look.

"I didn't answer him though," Maggie went on. She made a face. "All he ever wants to talk about is corporate law. The last date we had, I came right out and told him if he was going to talk about briefs, they'd better be the ones he had on under his trousers."

Laughing, Nick leaned against Katie. She stepped away, trying to concentrate on the conversation, something she always had difficulty doing when Nick was touching her. "I think it's wise to wait. After all, the party is still more than a week away. You never know what might happen."

"Well," Maggie sighed. "I can tell you one thing that won't happen: I won't get asked by the one man I want to go with."

"Why don't you ask him?" Nick suggested. "Maybe he's shy."

"Ask him?" she questioned in a thin voice as

she turned an unhealthy shade of gray. "Somehow, I don't think that would be a very good idea." She glanced at her oversize wristwatch, relief visibly washing over her. Her shoulders sagged. Even her hair seemed to relax. "Oh, my, just look at the time. Mrs. Pruitt will be waiting for me."

With a quick wave, she was out of the kitchen. Nick watched her until she had stepped out into the gray morning, then he turned back toward Katie. "You're gonna have to give that brother of yours a talking to."

"Me?" Katie asked, sifting through the recipes with interest. "You're a man. Why don't you talk to him?"

"You're a relative. There's less chance of him mortally wounding you." Giving Ryland Quaid advice on his love life did not seem like a healthy thing to do, Nick decided.

"I have every intention of speaking to Ry about it." Katie said. "And Maggie. I've never seen such foolishness. They shoot off their mouths at each other like a couple of machine guns—until the topic turns to romance. Then you can't make a half-wit out of the pair of them.

"What's *pollo del padrone*?" she asked, singling out a recipe card. "It sounds delicious."

Nick pulled the recipe cards out of her hands, set them aside, and pulled Katie into his arms. "Your education has been woefully inadequate, Miss Quaid. Speaking from a culinary standpoint, that is. How about social dance? Do you know one foot from the other, or am I going to have to give you a crash course before the big party?"

Katie frowned at him. "I told you once—I can't dance, Nick."

He hung on to her when she tried to step out of his arms. It was time Katie found out there were no absolutes. It seemed to Nick she perhaps had been too accepting of her limitations. Katie was no quitter, but she tended to see things only one way. It was time she found out there was more than one solution to every problem. If she would learn to compromise, she would be able to have many of the things she now denied herself. Dancing was one of those things, he knew. Children were another.

"Now, there's dancing, and then there's dancing," he said patiently.

Katie shook her head in frustration. "I can't. I

would love nothing more than to be able to dance with you at the party, but I can't."

"You thought you couldn't have a relationship with me either," he pointed out.

"That was different."

"No, it wasn't. You had it in your head no man was going to want you, and you wouldn't reconsider."

"Falling in love with you wasn't dangerous to my health," she argued. "My doctor says I can't dance. I can't dance."

"You are so stubborn!" He threw his hands in the air in exasperation. "If you would just listen to me, but no. You see things only one way—your way. Nobody else knows anything."

"I never said that!"

"But you're correct about this, right?"

"Yes."

"What do you think, I'm gonna ask you to do the samba and lift you over my head and spin you around? You think I'm gonna make you do the lindy or something?" By the expression on Katie's face he could tell she was stuck on remembering the turns and leaps he did in his Highwayman act. He forced himself to rein in his temper and cool off on a long sigh. Cradling Katie's face in his hands he looked deep into her eyes. "Do you trust me?"

"Yes," she whispered, feeling miserable. She trusted Nick, but she knew he didn't understand. He was the one who was being stubborn, not she.

"Good. Come upstairs with me."

"But—"

He silenced her with a warning look and a finger on her lips. Pulling Katie along behind him, he strode through the nearly finished main dining room, which was crowded with a haphazard arrangement of tables and chairs. They climbed the stairs, past the unfinished second floor, past his apartment, all the way up to the attic.

It looked very different from the first time Katie had seen it. It had been a dim, musty, cluttered place. Now gray light poured in through skylights on the north side of the peaked roof. The wood floor had been scrubbed and polished to a soft sheen. All the junk had been removed, leaving a long hollow space. Tucked back in one corner was a sophisticated stereo system. One wall was lined with mirrors. Along the wall opposite the mirrors sat a set of weights.

Nick abandoned Katie in the middle of the floor. While he put a tape on to play, she stood staring glumly at the Palladian window. Rain poured down so hard she could see nothing beyond the glass. Silver and opaque, it was like a sheet of mercury flowing over the panes. She felt alone, but then Nick was standing in front of her, gazing down at her with dark eyes silently begging for her trust.

He pointed to his ear. "Listen to the music," he said quietly. He pointed to his eyes. "Watch my eyes." He drew her hand to his heart. "Trust me." He took her in his arms as the music began.

It was a slow song. Sad. Sweet. Soft. And yet the sound wound around them, shutting out everything else, wrapping them in a cocoon where only the two of them existed—the two of them, the music, and love. Slowly they moved around the floor. Nick guided her, turned her, held her, all the while asking for her to trust him, telling her with his body and his eyes that she could trust him to lead her, that he would never let her go, never let anything hurt her.

He was strength and power, but now the strength, the power, the speed, the agility were leashed. It was his compromise for her. Hers was to relax in his arms, to follow him unquestioning.

They glided across the floor, around the empty room. In the mirrors along the wall Katie could see their reflection. They moved as one, two bodies in harmony. It was not unlike making love, she thought—a man's tempered strength, a woman's sweet, yielding trust. Certainly there was a fine line between the dance they were sharing and passion's dance.

Gradually, they crossed it.

As the music sang on, Nick deftly removed Katie's panties from under her skirt and lifted her against him. She was so tiny, so fragile, he thought, holding her close as he moved and turned. She made him feel strong, masculine, loved. He unzipped his pants with his right hand, holding Katie firmly with his left. He wanted to give her everything, to be everything for her.

He freed himself from his pants and she arched against him, her legs around his hips, her head thrown back as she took him into her warm, soft body. Her dark hair cascaded down behind her in a curtain of silk, swaying in time as they danced and loved. With one strong arm wrapped around

her, Nick brought his other hand around to free
her breasts so he could kiss them and caress them
and feast his eyes on their beauty in the pale silver
light of the room. He moved into her. She moved
over him. They clung and kissed and sighed as
their dance ended and ecstasy claimed them both.

"We're supposed to be getting ready to inter-
view prospective employees," Katie said as she
nuzzled into Nick's shoulder. They had moved
from his studio in the attic to his bedroom and
spent the rest of the morning making love, ignoring the work they had planned to do downstairs.
"That is why I took the afternoon off."

"Really?" he asked, stroking his hand down
her back and over her bottom. "I thought you
took the afternoon off so we could spend it in pur-
suit of carnal delights."

Katie nipped at his collarbone. "Think again,
Yankee. I'm here to make certain you don't hire
any sexy waitresses."

"How about sexy waiters?"

"They're okay," she said, raising up on one elbow. She looked down at him with a mischievous

smile as she played with a black curl that tumbled across his forehead. "In fact, I was thinking you should hire some of the guys from Hepplewhite's."

"Oh, really?" He lifted a dark brow in question.

"Sure. They could wait tables and do a floor show."

"You'd like that, would you? You'd like being able to watch a bunch of great-looking guys take their clothes off every night."

"Mmm, I think so," she speculated, trying not to grin at the glower Nick wore. "I had a lot of fun at Hepplewhite's. Next time I think I'll try giving one of the guys a tip in his G-string."

"Think again, Kathryn Quaid," he said, gently rolling her beneath him, tangling them both in the sheet. "The only G-string I want you playing with is mine."

Katie giggled as he attacked her throat with kisses. "Jealous?" she managed to ask.

"Insanely," he said on a groan as he slid into her.

The interviews dragged on through the afternoon with a seemingly endless number of qualified and not-so-qualified people applying for positions. Nick found the whole process fascinating. He loved meeting people. No two were exactly alike. Still, after a couple of hours, his attention began to wander in Katie's direction—and hers began to wander his way.

She slipped her pumps off under the table and ran her foot up and down his calf while he tried to ask a pimply-faced teenager if he would be able to wash dishes on weekends. Between interviews, they discussed the people they'd seen, pretending to be businesslike while their gazes locked and heated. By the time the last prospective employee walked out the front door, they were on the verge of spontaneous combustion.

They rose slowly from their chairs, stretching, pretending indifference. Then Nick pulled Katie into his arms and kissed her, and all thoughts of indifference were vaporized. He kissed her as if he were starving and she was the only form of sustenance on earth. She gripped at his shoulders for support, the fabric of his shirt bunching in her fists. Her head swam as desire dragged her under.

How could it be possible to want him so badly when they'd spent the entire morning tending each other's physical needs, Katie wondered dimly. As soon as she asked herself the question, she knew she didn't care what the answer was. The wild, insatiable hunger she felt was part of loving Nick. That was all she needed to know.

"How can I need you this much?" he asked, on the verge of desperation as he tore his mouth from hers. He only wanted her more as he looked down at her. Her prim summer dress was wrinkled from his hands on her shoulders; her soft, soft mouth was red and slick from his kiss. "Let's go upstairs."

Katie filled her lungs with air, hoping to steady herself a little. "I have to go over to the store for a few minutes. I'll come right back."

"Good," Nick said, calmer with a few inches of space between them. "I'll cook us a nice dinner."

"I'm going to get fat from all your nice dinners."

"Not a chance, kitten." He gave her a lazy, predatory smile. "We'll work it off later."

Remarkably, she blushed as she turned and headed for the door.

Nick shook his head as he watched her go. Sometimes Katie was like a young girl—all blushes and giggles. More often she was a woman who was very sure of herself and her abilities. Then sometimes, when she thought he wasn't looking, shadows came into her eyes, and she looked so alone, it frightened him.

He pulled his glasses off, dropped them on the table beside the stack of applications, and rubbed the bridge of his nose. They had overcome two big obstacles in their relationship—his career as a stripper and her scars. There was one more obstacle they needed to overcome, and it was a big one. Nick wanted Katie in his life on a permanent basis, but he wanted their future to include children. He already knew he was going to have a fight on his hands to convince Katie to compromise.

A sound from the front door drew Nick's attention, and he gladly traded the possibility of trouble for the prospect of having Katie all to himself for the evening.

"That didn't take long," he said. The grin froze on his face as he turned and saw Rylan Quaid's figure looming in the doorway. "Ry. Good to see you. What brings you here?"

Ry shifted uncomfortably from one booted foot to the other. He clutched a battered blue baseball cap in front of him and looked about as happy as a brown shoe in a room full of tuxedos. His dark brows were pulled low over his eyes in his characteristic scowl. "Katie tells me you're a pretty good dancer."

It took an effort for Nick to push from his mind thoughts of the dancing he and Katie had done earlier. Hoping he didn't look too guilty, he tried to nod and shrug at the same time.

"Uh—do you reckon you could—uh—teach me to waltz?"

The impulse to burst into hysterical laughter was almost too much for him, but Nick held himself in rigid check. He could see what it had cost Ry to ask. The last thing he wanted to do was laugh at the man. To gain control, he glanced down at the job applications on the table, then he turned back to Ry, acting as if it were a question big, strapping men asked him every day. "Sure, no problem."

Ry nodded. He sighed in resignation, rubbing the back of his thick, sunburned neck. "Well, hell, let's do it, then, and get it over with."

* * *

Katie crossed the street with a bouncy step, smiling as if she deserved all the credit for Maggie's happiness. Ry finally had rounded up enough courage to ask her to the party. She couldn't wait to tell Nick.

He was nowhere to be found on the first floor of the restaurant. She leaned against the banister at the foot of the stairs, a slow smile spreading across her face as she heard the faint strains of music coming from above. It was a waltz—slow, sweet, wonderfully romantic. Nick had shown her she could dance with him. It sounded as if he was ready to give her another lesson.

Katie mounted the final steps to the attic, ready and willing to have Nick take her into his arms. But Nick's arms were already full—overflowing, in fact. She pressed a hand to her mouth to suppress her giggles at the sight of Nick waltzing around the room with Rylan.

Ry was scowling in concentration and shuffling his big, clumsy feet. Nick was trying to look encouraging, biting his lip every few steps when he couldn't quite escape a close encounter with size-thirteen cowboy boots.

"You're doing great," he said as he let Ry attempt to lead.

"You think so?"

"Oh, sure. You're really light on your feet." And heavy on mine, his grimace seemed to say. "Let's try the turn again. One, two, three. One, two, three."

They stepped uncertainly through the turn just as the music ended. Polite applause drew their attention in Katie's direction.

"You make a lovely couple," she said, straight-faced.

TEN

PERHAPS IN ITS younger days the Drewes mansion had looked as it did now, Katie thought as Nick helped her from the car and strolled with her up the walk. Beautiful. Alive with activity. But somehow, she was sure it had never looked quite so happy, quite so proud. It had been rescued from ruin and lovingly tended by people who were dedicated to preserving its heritage. Two hundred years ago it had been one of the finest houses in Virginia. Finally it was again. Katie was filled with a warm glow of pride and satisfaction.

She smiled up at Nick. "Can't you almost picture the guests who would have come here when the house was new? Men in satin breeches and velvet coats. Women with their powdered hair piled high, their elegant gowns swirling over layers and layers of petticoats. Men such as Thomas Jefferson and George Washington."

Nick laughed. "Don't tell me Washington slept here too." Nearly every town he'd been to in Virginia boasted of at least one visit from the father of the country.

"He did indeed," Katie answered, stopping on the path to face him. "And Madison and Monroe and Harrison. The Virginia gentry was a very close-knit community."

Nick drew her into his arms and smiled down at her. "Do you realize your face positively glows when you talk about the past? You're such a romantic, Kathryn."

As he would have predicted, she blushed and pretended to be annoyed by his remark. Heaven forbid anyone should think she was anything but the level-headed businesswoman. "Oh, pooh," she scoffed, picking an imaginary piece of lint off the lapel of his tux. "I'm just a history buff, that's all."

Nick chuckled and pressed a quick kiss to her forehead. "Stubborn. Shall we go in? I can't wait to see all the men drooling over you in this dress," he said just dryly enough to hint at jealousy. He wouldn't mind other men looking, so long as Katie stayed on his arm. He shot her a questioning glance. "Is it dark green?"

"No," Katie said with a laugh, shaking her head. "It's dark red."

"Gorgeous is what it is."

She smoothed a hand over the fabric of her skirt, a self-satisfied smile tilting her lips. She had turned the stores around D.C. upside down looking for the dress. It was burgundy-colored silk. The style was the ultimate in simplicity—thin straps over the shoulders, a deep vee in back that ended a safe inch above the scars from her back surgery. The bodice was a second skin that arrowed down over her stomach. The skirt fell from soft gathers, two whisper-thin layers ending in long fingerlike petals that swirled around her calves. She wore her hair up in an intricate knot of braids, and she looked as much like a princess as any woman Nick had ever seen.

The house overflowed with guests and enthusiasm. Everyone seemed to be talking and laughing at once as they mingled and moved through the elegantly restored mansion, while the chamber orchestra played Bach in the front parlor. The place was a sea of black and white tuxedos liberally splashed with the brilliant hues of evening gowns. Waiters decked out in colonial-style livery circulated through the crowd with silver trays of champagne glasses. The scent of expensive perfume mingled with the soft fragrance from the elaborate arrangements of fresh-cut flowers that graced the tables in each room.

At the foot of the grand staircase the president of the Society for the Preservation of Virginia Antiquities took Katie by the arm and congratulated her on a job well done.

"Thank you, Mrs. Byrd." Katie smiled at the older woman in the ruffled pink dress. "But I certainly didn't do this on my own. I was just a helper."

Mrs. Byrd gave her a sideways look with shrewd green eyes. "I know you, Kathryn. You're no simple worker bee. My spies tell me you were the one who persuaded the town to take this project on. Be modest if you will, but I intend to give credit where it's due."

Katie looked embarrassed. Nick nearly popped a stud on his shirt, he was so proud of her.

The ballroom was beautiful. Housed in its own wing off the south side of the house, it had French doors running the length of the room on either side of the polished wood floor. People wandered in and out through the open doors to the gardens. The band had set up at the far end of the room and played at a volume that allowed people to hold conversations without shouting. Around the perimeter of the room groups of three and four people stood chatting and sipping champagne. A small crowd had gathered on the dance floor to shuffle and sway to a slow tune from the twenties.

Exchanging a meaningful look, Nick and Katie headed straight for the dancers. He was careful with her. Careful not to turn too quickly, careful not to let other dancers bump into her, careful to keep the steps slow and simple. Nick was such an accomplished dancer, his caution wasn't notice-able. No one in the room knew he was holding back for Katie's sake—except Katie. She pushed the thought from her mind, too happy to let it spoil her mood.

She focused instead on Nick himself. He was breathtaking in a tux, his dark good looks intensified by the white of his shirt and the sharp styling of his jacket. She remembered how he had looked in his attic-turned-studio, in a T-shirt and jeans with the white, sunless light falling on him through the rain-spattered window. She remembered the eloquent plea for trust in his brown velvet eyes. She had given him her trust, and he had given her the chance to move and float, to dance when she had been so sure she would never be able to. Her heart swelled with love for him.

As they made their way around the floor they spotted Ry and Maggie. Maggie wore a pained smile and a strapless dress of black charmeuse. Ry was moving with all the grace of a dancing bear. He looked distinctly unhappy in a tuxedo, as if he were afraid to breathe too deeply for fear the seams of his jacket would split. Katie's heart went out to him. She knew how nervous he had been about dancing.

"Relax a little bit, will you?" Nick whispered

to him when the song was over and the four of them gravitated toward the punch bowl.

"I hate this damn suit," Rylan grumbled, scowling. He ran a thick finger along the inside of the starched collar of his white shirt, swallowing uncomfortably. "Trussed up like a rump roast on Easter Sunday. Cripes. They must've saved these shoes from the Spanish Inquisition. They couldn't hurt any worse if the farrier had nailed them to my feet with big iron spikes."

"Just cool out, will you?" Nick said, patting Ry's massive shoulder with brotherly affection. "Have a glass of punch and wait for a waltz. You're doing fine. Just remember to listen to the music and relax."

Maggie leaned toward Katie. "I'm afraid to look. Do I still have two feet? I could have sworn he ground one right into the floor during that last song."

Katie bit her lip and gave her friend a pleading look. "Be patient with him, Mary Margaret. He's trying so hard."

"Sugar, if he tries any harder, he's liable to kill me." She glanced at Ry as he picked up two glasses of pink punch, and sent him a smile. He spilled half a glass and scowled at the serving girl as if it were her fault. "Don't ask me what I see in him. He's surly and churlish and sarcastic. We bicker constantly and never agree on anything." A soft sigh slipped through lips that had been painted ruby red. The light in her brown eyes softened. "He's a handsome devil in that tux, though, isn't he?"

Katie reserved comment. Handsome was not a word most people used to describe Ry. It was too tame and pretty a word for him. Rugged was probably the most polite thing she'd heard him called, but Maggie thought he was handsome. They were an unlikely pair, her big scowling brother and her social-butterfly best friend. For some reason Katie thought their differences made them all the more perfect for each other.

While the band took a break, the four of them stood on the sidelines enjoying the breeze that drifted in through one of the French doors, bringing in the rich scents of the garden and the warm Virginia evening. Conversation centered on the house, the party, the people in attendance. Ry and Maggie bantered back and forth in their usual fashion, Ry having left all his shyness about dating his sister's best friend out on the dance floor. Zoe and Darrell Baylor joined them. Zoe was stunning in an electric-blue sheath. Darrell wore the required tuxedo and his usual pleasant smile.

"Evening everybody," he said in greeting. "It's a lovely party, even if it's not exciting enough for my wife."

Zoe gaped at him. "I never said that!"

Darrell gave her an innocent look. "You said the tourism committee would have done better if they'd skipped the orchestra and hired those male dancers from Hepplewhite's."

Everyone laughed while Zoe made an embarrassed face. She shook a finger at her husband. "Just you wait until we get home."

Darrell lifted a brow above the gold rim of his glasses. "Are you going to make me dress up like the Highwayman again?"

Katie and Nick exchanged an amused look while the others teased Zoe mercilessly.

Looking off across the room Katie's gaze settled on a woman who could have walked right off the cover of *Vogue*. Black hair skimmed angular shoulders and framed an oval face. Katie had a feeling the emerald-green dress the woman wore probably matched the color of her eyes. "Who's that with Doll Harris?"

"That's John's niece from New Orleans," Maggie said, sipping her punch. "Jayne Sutton. She's visiting for a few weeks. Lost her husband several months back. She's awfully nice, and if she doesn't have the most darlin' baby girl, I don't know who does. She writes and illustrates children's books—Jayne, that is."

"Jeepers cripes, Mary Margaret, why don't you just write a book?" Ry asked in his sarcastic drawl.

Maggie narrowed her eyes at him and discreetly tugged up the slipping bodice of her strapless dress. "Some people like to keep up on what's going on around them, Rylan."

They were joined then by the Harrises and their niece. Jayne Sutton was exactly as Maggie had said—nice. Friendly and outgoing, everyone liked her instantly. One minute introductions were being made, the next Jayne was inviting everyone to a picnic in Donner Park. She seemed to have an innate ability to put people at ease and treat strangers as if they were lifelong friends.

As the orchestra swung into a forties big-band number, the couples moved back out to the dance floor. Maggie even managed to tug Ry off the sidelines.

Jayne's toe began tapping to the bouncy beat as she watched the couples dancing. "I love this old jitterbug stuff." She grinned at Katie and Nick and motioned them out to the crowded floor. "You two should be out there dancing up a storm."

Nick felt Katie's shoulder stiffen under his hand. She kept a smile in place as she said, "Not me. I couldn't move that fast if my life depended on it." She looked up at Nick and felt as if she were plunging a knife into her own heart. "Why don't you ask Jayne to dance?"

A fist of tension knotted in Nick's stomach. Why would she suggest such a thing? Deep in her gray eyes he could see hurt and sadness hiding behind her phony smile, and a ribbon of foreboding snaked through him. He felt her pushing him away—emotionally, then physically, as she put a hand on his arm.

"Go on, Nick. I'm sure Jayne would enjoy it."

Jayne looked as confused as Nick felt. Uncertainly she said, "If you're sure you don't mind."

"Don't be silly," Katie said brightly. "It's only a dance. Why would I mind?"

Only a masochist wouldn't have minded, Katie told herself as she watched Nick and Jayne head for the dance floor. It was the worst kind of torture to stand there and watch the man she loved dancing with the woman she could never be. They made a striking couple—tall and athletic, grinning and laughing as they negotiated the quick steps and turns of the jitterbug. Nick was graceful, his movements a fluid blend of instinct and instruction. Jayne was less certain of herself but full of enthusiasm and determined to keep up with her partner. Nick didn't have to be careful with her.

Katie suddenly felt as if she had three left feet— all of them flat. She felt puny and slow... and hollow—a feeling she hadn't experienced since before her first night of lovemaking with Nick. He had made her feel like a whole woman. But she wasn't.

He was a healthy, active man, a man with a talent she could never fully share and dreams she could never fulfill. What right did she have to keep him from them?

The dance ended with a flourish on the drums. Nick spun Jayne around so hard her dress twirled around her legs. They came back to Katie breathless and happy.

"Oh...that was...fun," Jayne declared between gasps as she combed her hair back out of her eyes. She gave Katie's shoulders a friendly squeeze. "Thanks for lending him to me, Katie."

"Anytime," Katie said, earning her a perplexed look from Nick.

As Jayne made her way toward the punch bowl, Nick slipped his arms around Katie from behind and dipped his head down next to hers. "Are you feeling okay?"

"I'm fine. My back's a little sore, is all." She couldn't have said which was the bigger lie.

Nick brushed a kiss against her temple, concerned. Katie never complained about aches and pains even though he knew she had them. In fact, she always had been stubbornly determined not to mention them to him. "You want to go home? I'll give you a back rub."

"No," she said absently, watching Jayne tilt her head and laugh at something Zoe Baylor said. "I'll be fine. Jayne is awfully nice, don't you think?"

"Yeah, she's nice," he replied in an offhand tone. He wanted to get away from the subject of Jayne Sutton, because he had a feeling it wasn't just Jayne they were discussing. Even now, with Katie in his arms, he could feel her pulling away, going into that little room inside herself and closing the door between them. Something had upset her. No doubt the fact that she hadn't been able to dance the swing number with him. He still didn't understand why she had pushed him to dance with Jayne instead. He wasn't sure he wanted to understand.

What he wanted was to bring Katie back to him—the laughing, smiling Katie he had brought to the party. He hated it when she distanced herself from him. Whether she knew it or not, she took a part of him with her when she went and left him feeling empty and alone. He hadn't been looking for love when he'd met Katie, but he'd

found it. She colored all his thoughts, all his perceptions. Most of the time it was an exhilarating
thing. When she pulled away from him, it was
scary.

"Let's go out in the garden," he suggested.
Without waiting to hear her opinion, he headed in
that direction with Katie in tow. Avoiding the
other couples who had come outside for a breath
of fresh air, he led her down the worn brick path.
When he found the corner farthest from the
house, he leaned back against the low wall and
pulled Katie into his arms.

She went willingly, feeling tired and drained. It
was nice to stand against Nick, to lean on his
solid strength, to breathe in his warm, clean scent.
She leaned against him and cleared her mind until
there was nothing in it but the night with its sliver
of moon and shower of stars, the garden, rich
with fragrance, and Nick.

Nick slowly slid his hand back and forth across
her bare shoulders as he stared out into the night,
willing them both to relax. Finally he asked Katie,
"Why did you want me to dance with Jayne
Sutton?"

She wasn't quite ready to discover the real answer to that question herself, so she gave him the most logical one instead. "She wanted to dance. You wanted to dance. Neither of you had a partner."

"I had a partner," he corrected. "And you never bothered asking me if I wanted to dance. Maybe I didn't want to. Maybe I wanted just to stand with you and enjoy the music."

Loyalty. It was one of his strongest virtues. And one of his biggest faults, Katie thought. "Dance with the girl you brung. Leave on the horse you rode in on," she murmured.

"What the hell is that supposed to mean?"

"Nothing. Don't pay any attention to me. I guess I'm just feeling sorry for myself. I know how much you love to dance, and I wanted to be able to dance with you."

"You did dance with me."

"You know what I mean."

He cupped her stubborn chin in his hand and tilted her face up. "I know Kathryn Quaid is the lady who made this evening possible. I know she's the one who worked like a demon to save this magnificent old house. I know she has the respect not only of her friends and neighbors, but also of a great many other people." His smile went from gentle to teasing in the blink of an eye. "All that and you want to be able to jitterbug too? You're a greedy woman."

Greedy for him. She wanted everything for Nick. It wasn't that she couldn't live the rest of her life without playing Ginger Rogers. Katie had accepted her limitations. But she wanted to shed them for Nick. He had given her so much. Why should he have to settle for less than everything in return?

"It's not that important to me, Katie," he said, as if he had read her thoughts. "Dancing isn't the most important part of my life anymore. You are."

Telling her with words wasn't enough. He told her with his kiss as well. Long, deep, just a little desperate, as if he were afraid she wouldn't believe him. When he lifted his mouth from hers, his breathing was as unsteady as his heartbeat.

"You know," he said, struggling to give her a smile that would offset the tension that had seeped into his kiss, "I've always thought the jitterbug was highly overrated. What we were doing in my attic—now *that* was a dance, my favorite dance."

Katie smiled in remembrance, pushing away the melancholy mood that had settled over her like a damp cloak. There was no sense in ruining the evening mourning things that could never be. It was better to enjoy the evening and make memories she could store away in a satin-lined box in her heart, memories she could take out later to fill an empty night. She reached up and brushed back a lock of black hair that had tumbled onto his forehead. "That was my favorite dance too."

"So maybe we should save our energy for later," he suggested, running his hand down her back, loving the feel of her warm, smooth skin where her dress left her exposed, "when we can have a dance floor all to ourselves."

She nodded against his chest. "For now, we should go back in and make sure Ry hasn't trampled Maggie into the floor."

Nick pretended offense. "Is that an insult to my abilities as a dance instructor?"

"No, it's an insult to Ry's abilities as a dance student." She slid her arm around his waist and hugged him as they walked back toward the light and noise of the party. "I have no complaints about the way you taught me how to dance."

"Ry didn't get the same kind of personal treatment."

"Thank heaven," she said dryly.

ELEVEN

IT WAS A perfect summer day. The sky was cloudless, the sun unyielding, but a merciful breeze kissed the skin, and the humidity, which so often smothered Virginia in summer, had taken the day off. It was the kind of day tailor-made for picnics in the park.

For Katie, a picnic in the park with her friends and their families was a bittersweet experience. She would enjoy their company but sit on the sidelines and watch while the others jumped and stumbled and sweated their way through a game of volleyball. She would enjoy the meal and the talk but would sit in isolation while they tended children with empty tummies, tummy aches, and skinned knees. For Nick it would be a fun, relaxing afternoon. For Katie it would be a reminder of everything she had lost and could never regain.

In the dark hours before dawn she had lain beside him thinking while he slept. She'd never been so happy as she was with Nick. She'd never felt more complete, more feminine, more loved. Weeks before she would have told herself she deserved all those things. She would have hung on to him. Something had changed inside her since then. There had been a subtle shift in her feelings. They had deepened and grown into something she couldn't grasp with a greedy hand. When she had watched him dance with Jayne Sutton, she hadn't felt jealousy, she had only wondered at her own right to hold him back.

How happy could he be with her and for how long? He wanted a family. She knew what that felt like. She had longed for one herself. But she couldn't give him a child of his own, and she didn't know if she could face the alternative. Adoption. People offered the piece of advice so quickly, so cavalierly. Perhaps for some people it was that simple. Perhaps they'd never dug deeply enough to uncover the fears she had.

Katie wasn't—had never been—the kind of woman who wanted to mother everyone's children. She had never begged to hold a baby, had never automatically scooped up a toddler for a hug. It was true, she had wanted a family, but what if there was something lacking in her, and she simply wasn't capable of loving a child not of her own making? What if she were given a child who could have gone to someone more deserving? What if her motives were wrong? What if she were adopting a child simply to prove she could outdo her own mother or to make up for her own childhood? What if she turned out to be just as poor a mother as her own mother had been? How could she put a child through that?

Compromise, Nick preached. She could compromise on some issues, not on others. The real question was, should Nick be expected to compromise? If she couldn't accept adoption, would he be willing to give up his dream of a family? Loving him the way she did, could she ask that of him?

In the dark, lonely hours of the night, when

there was nowhere for the truth to hide, the answer to her question was no.

"This is gonna be great," Nick said with a grin as he popped the hatch on his Trans Am. He lifted the cooler out of the trunk, set it on the ground, and turned back to get the picnic basket. "You know, when the restaurant opens I won't be able to take many days off. We'll have to make the most of this one, won't we, kitten?"

Katie smiled distractedly. "Yes, we will."

She planned to make the most of it. She planned to soak up his presence, to memorize his every expression and the sound of his voice. Nick didn't realize how precious their afternoon together was going to be. It was going to be their last.

"Are you sure you packed the container of shrimp salad in here?" He was bent over, digging through the cooler.

Katie hooked a finger through a belt loop on his cutoffs and tugged. "You know I did. You watched me put it in. You're just looking for an excuse to dig out a beer."

"You know me too well," he said chuckling, straightening with a sweating can of the brew in one hand. His gaze swept down her appreciatively, taking in her lightweight cotton tank top and soft blue peasant skirt. Even though she had grown comfortable with him seeing her scars, she still refused to let anyone else see them. That was why she wore a skirt when everyone else would be in shorts. Nick didn't complain though. He thought the way she dressed only enhanced her delicate feminine beauty. He wrapped his arm around her and pulled her close for a quick kiss.

Maggie's voice called out to them from the picnic site. "Hey, you lovebirds, no necking in the park!"

"Jealous?" Nick questioned as he hoisted the cooler onto the picnic table beside her.

Maggie slid her sunglasses down her nose and batted her eyelashes at him. "Is that an offer, Yankee?"

Nick shot a look at Ry. "You gotta do something about her, Quaid."

Ry tipped his baseball cap back and wiped the sweat from his forehead with the back of his hand. "Aw, hell," he said. "Just feed her something an' she'll leave you alone."

"Rylan Quaid, you haven't the manners God gave a goat!" Maggie yanked the bill of his cap down over his face and turned away with her nose in the air, pretending offense at his teasing. "I declare, I don't know why I'd want to go anywhere with you."

Ry shoved his cap back into place and grinned at her. " 'Cause I'm a great kisser."

Much to everyone's amusement, Maggie's face turned as red as her hair. Katie smiled to herself. She was happy to see the romance of her brother and her best friend progressing, even if her own relationship was nearing an end.

The afternoon passed with the laziness peculiar to summer in the South. Food was eaten, beer and soda poured down parched throats. The adults sprawled in lawn chairs or on blankets, digesting their dinner and soaking up the sun and the latest gossip.

Katie soaked up the experience. Because she was more in tune with Nick, she was more in tune with everything: the way the breeze stirred the leaves, the scent of grilling meat, the way Zoe smiled at her husband, the sound of Haley Sutton, Jayne's daughter, cooing as she played on a blanket beneath an oak tree.

She was almost painfully aware of Nick. She studied the play of sun and shadow on the angular planes of his dark face. Her gaze drifted down the long, beautiful length of his body as he stretched on the quilt. He moved with all the sinuous grace of a big cat. There wasn't an inch of him she didn't know on intimate terms.

"Volleyball time!" Darrell Baylor announced, taking the ball from his son and spinning it on the top of his index finger.

"It's the only trick he knows," Zoe explained as she headed for the volleyball court, which was nothing more than a net and an area marked off by faded white chalk lines on the grass.

Maggie and Ry went to the court arguing about who would beat who.

"You women stand about as much chance of winning as I do of becoming Miss America."

"You're full of hot air, Quaid," Maggie said. "We're gonna cream you. Zoe and I will have Nick on our team. Right, Nick?"

"Maybe." Nick sat up on the quilt and brushed

a lock of Katie's hair back from her face. "You mind if I play?"

She shook her head, mustering a benign smile. "No, of course not. You go on. I'll cheer for you." It would have been nice to keep him by her side all day, but she wanted to see him active and happy. Somehow, Katie thought, that would make the break easier.

He gave her a kiss, shed his red T-shirt, and went to join the others.

Katie watched him jog away, trying to stem the flow of longing. She'd done a good job of hiding her emotions so far. Nick, who was usually acutely attuned to her moods, didn't seem suspicious in the least.

As the game began, Katie rose and went to the table where Jayne was supervising while her daughter mangled a hot dog.

"Not playing?" Jayne asked, glancing over her shoulder. She turned back just in time to intercept part of Haley's dinner, which the little girl had tried to throw to Watch.

"No. I thought I might take a walk." She offered her dog a piece of biscuit and watched Jayne persuade Haley to eat another bite of meat. The little girl was going to have her mother's looks and sunny disposition. "She's a beautiful little girl. You're very lucky."

With a wistful expression on her face, Jayne brushed a ladybug from her daughter's black hair. "Yes, I am."

Katie stood for a moment longer. She watched as Jayne tried to wipe mustard off Haley's face. The baby wailed in protest as she turned her head from side to side in an attempt to avoid her mother's ministrations. On the volleyball court, Maggie closed her eyes and blindly swung at the ball Rylan had bumped her way. Nick dove for it but missed and ended up rolling in the grass, tackling Reese Baylor. The little boy's shrieks of delight as Nick tickled him rang out above the laughter of the adults. Nick sat up, his black hair tousled, his crooked grin lighting up his face, his arms wrapped around Reese in an exuberant hug.

I'm doing the right thing, Katie told herself, the best thing for Nick. And, while she felt an overwhelming sadness, she also felt at peace with herself. With her hands tucked into the pockets of her skirt, she turned and started walking, her dog reluctantly trailing behind her.

She was almost to the statue of the unknown Confederate war dead when Nick saw her out of the corner of his eye. At first he wanted to deny it was Katie walking away, even though it had to be her. His gaze made a quick reconnaissance of the picnic site before returning to the small figure headed east and the enormous gray dog that trudged along behind her.

"Hey, Leone, you gonna serve that ball or not?" Ry called from across the court.

"Not," Nick mumbled absently. He dropped the ball and jogged after Katie with a strange feeling crawling around in his stomach. Why would she be walking away? Why would she want to leave without telling him? Had he gotten too caught up in the activities and ignored her?

"Katie!"

She stopped at the sound of her name but didn't turn around. She hadn't planned on telling him there, but it was as good a time as any, she thought as the sound of Nick's sneakers pounding on the hard ground drew near. She would tell him now, get it over with, and go home. He ran past her a step and stopped, then pivoted to face her.

Although he smiled, his expression was one of concern.

"Where do you think you're going without telling me?"

"Home," she said simply.

She didn't look angry. She looked... tired, resigned. The uneasiness inside him hardened into a cold lump. "Why? Was I too caught up in the game? 'Cause if that's it, I'll just—"

"No," Katie said in a quiet, unflappable tone. "You were enjoying yourself. I don't begrudge you that, Nick. I want you to enjoy yourself. I don't want you sitting on the sidelines just because I have to."

He sighed a little impatiently and planted his hands on his hips. "It's because of the kids, isn't it?"

"No. Not in the way you mean."

Because he was looking for a reason he could latch on to and argue about with her, he didn't want to believe her denial. But he knew she was telling the truth. If anything, she had been more at ease with the children than he had ever seen her. There still had been shadows in her eyes, she still had held back a part of herself, but she had talked with Reese, had helped Charisse color. He had even seen her holding Jayne Sutton's baby. And the word *resignation* came back to him again. She had seemed resigned, as if she had given up on trying to distance herself.

Instead of being glad of it, Nick felt nervous.

"You just want to go home?" he asked. "Let's pack up, then, and take the car."

"No."

There was a finality in her tone he didn't want to hear. Dodging her gaze he lifted his shoulders in a shrug. "Okay, so we'll walk."

"No, Nick. I'm going home alone."

"What are you saying?"

Years of teaching herself cool composure stood Katie in good stead. Yet she felt as if she were cutting the words she had to say right out of her soul. She might have been able to meet Nick's demanding gaze head-on, but that didn't make what she had to do any easier. "It's over, Nick. I'm doing what's best: I'm letting you go."

Stunned was the only word to describe his initial reaction. He'd felt Katie pulling back, but he hadn't expected her to react so drastically. He'd sensed the previous night that something was bothering her, but he'd assumed the problem had been a minor one. She'd been upset about not being able to dance—that wasn't something people broke up over. After the party they had gone back to Katie's house and spent most of the night making the sweetest love he'd ever known—that wasn't something a woman did right before she told a guy to take a hike.

Unless she'd been saying good-bye to him. Unless she'd been making memories to store against a future without him.

I'm doing what's best: I'm letting you go.

Anger surfaced over his surprise. "Who the hell is that supposed to be best for?"

It cut deep to see the hurt and confusion on his face. Katie would have done anything to spare him pain. But a little hurt now was nothing compared to ruining his life, she reminded herself. It was better to force him out of her life now than see him miserable, staying with her out of loyalty later on. Nick deserved to get everything he wanted out of life. If that meant she had to leave him now, she would do it. She had known it wouldn't be easy, but she would survive. Loving Nick had been like a glimpse of heaven, beautiful and unexpected.

She was glad for it, even if it had been only a glimpse.

"It's best for you," she said. Oh, how she wanted to reach out and touch him, to try to ease the hurt, but she forced herself to hold back. "Nick, you deserve more than I can give you. You deserve someone who's strong and whole, someone like Jayne Sutton."

The only defense he could muster was sarcasm. He laughed without a trace of humor. "You got somebody all picked out for me. That's big of you, Kathryn."

"I didn't say it had to be Jayne," she clarified with a calm that antagonized his temper. "Just someone like Jayne, someone who can dance with you and play with you and give you the family you've always wanted."

"I've told you dancing isn't important to me, Katie. I love the things we do together, the quiet things. And if I feel the need to do something more physical, I can do it on my own. It's not as if we're joined at the hip. And what makes you think I have to have a family?" he asked, knowing it was a stupid question but being too desperate to care. "I'm thirty-two. I sure as hell could've started one by now."

"That first day you came to the Drewes mansion you said so. You said you loved kids and that someday you'd have a dozen."

He swore at her excellent memory and the fact that he had apparently cut his own throat with a casual remark. Yes, he wanted a family, but he wanted Katie first. "You should have read me my rights at the beginning: Anything I say can and will be used against me in the court of Quaid."

Katie stubbornly ignored his anger. She wasn't intimidated by him even if his expression was close to savage. His dark brows slashed down over brown eyes burning with pent-up fury. The mouth that could so easily lift into a boyish grin was twisted into a thin, cynical line. He felt helpless, he was lashing out—she understood the combination well. "I know you want children, Nick, and there's no reason you shouldn't have them. I certainly don't intend to stand in your way."

"No, you intend to push me out of yours. Get me out of your way so you can go back to feeling sorry for yourself."

He could have slapped her and it would have

hurt less. She didn't try to deny his words, though, even if she didn't feel she deserved them. It was better to have him angry with her. The break would be easier.

Nick swore silently and the words were directed at himself. He had never meant to be vindictive. He didn't mean it, but there was no taking the words back now. If he was lucky, they would rouse a spark of anger in Katie and burn through her resolve to let him go.

But she didn't snap back at him. She looked as if she were simply waiting for him to step off the path so she could go home. She looked sad. She looked resigned. For the first time he felt a stab of real fear that he was going to lose her.

"So what happens," he asked, "when I find the perfect woman you want for me and it turns out I'm sterile? Can I have you back then? Is infertility the one thing we need to have in common for me to keep you in my life?"

She wouldn't have guessed he considered it a small victory that she both sounded and looked annoyed when she answered him. "Don't be ridiculous."

"Ridiculous? You think it couldn't happen?

You think you're the only person on earth who can't have children?"

"Of course not," she said, trying to rein in her frustration. Why couldn't he see she was doing him a favor? "But chances are you're perfectly able. You deserve——"

"I deserve to have the woman I love," he said. If she understood nothing else, she had to know he loved her. His love had to count for something. "Maybe I have always wanted a family. That's not a crime. But the first thing I need is the woman I love. Katie, if I don't have you, I'll never have anything. I've never felt the way you make me feel. You think I should give that up and go looking for something else?"

"Yes," she said without hesitation. Her mind was made up. She wasn't going to let him talk her out of it with words of love and the sincere expression in his dark eyes.

"Shouldn't it be my decision to make?"

She felt the need again, the need to reach out to him. If she could touch him, perhaps she could make him understand. But if she touched him, she would be lost. So she tried to touch him, to convince him, with her expression, with her heart in her eyes. "Maybe, but I think you're too good a man to make it."

"Oh, Katie..." he said on a long sigh, shaking his head. He dragged a hand back through his hair. She wasn't going to listen to reason. He may as well have been talking to the statue of the unknown Confederate war dead. "Why does it have to be all or nothing with you? There are compromises. If you'd stop being so pigheaded, we could work this out—"

"You think I don't know about compromises?" she asked. "That's all my life has been for the last five years. All I've done is make compromises."

"And you've made all the wrong ones. Letting go of all your dreams isn't a compromise, it's giving up. We can work this through together, honey. You just have to be willing to try. You thought your scars made you undesirable. You were wrong. You thought you couldn't even try to dance with me. You were wrong. You think you can't have a family. You could be wrong about that too."

"I'm not."

"You are so damn stubborn!" He slammed his fist against the rough trunk of a persimmon tree and welcomed the distraction of the brief explosion of pain.

Katie didn't need to strike anything to feel pain. What she was feeling inside was bad enough. "I'm realistic," she said. "Do you think I haven't considered the options? Do you really think I haven't gone over them, that I just blindly decided adoption isn't for me?"

"I think you've probably exhausted all arguments on the topic. I think you've been over it until you've blinded yourself to everything but your own fears."

Ignoring the ring of truth in his statement she closed her eyes and muttered to herself, "This is pointless." She looked up at him. "Nick, you're just proving me right. I can't give you what you want."

This was it. This was going to be the end. He could see it in her pewter-colored eyes. It was there right beside regret. Wearily he fought against his own sense of resignation. He didn't want to give her up, but the choice didn't seem to be his to make. He reached out a hand to touch her cheek with the very tips of his fingers.

"Katie," he asked. He pulled his lower lip between his teeth for an instant. One last try. "Do you love me?"

"Yes." She whispered because she didn't trust her voice not to break. Oh, yes, she loved him. She loved him more than she had ever dreamed possible. She loved him wholly. She loved him unselfishly. And because her love had deepened from possessive to unselfish, she had to let him go.

A cold wave washed over Nick, defying the heat of the afternoon. Tears pressed against the backs of his eyes with an unfamiliar pressure. He had to talk around a knot of them in his throat. "Katie, if you love me, you won't go."

Finally she gave in to the need to touch him— just once, just one last time. Echoing his gesture, she lifted a hand and pressed her fingertips against his lean cheek. His skin was smooth in spite of the shadow of his beard. She caught a lone tear on the tip of her finger and drew back from him.

"Because I love you, I have to do this."

She stepped around him and started down the worn dirt path. Panic washed through Nick as he watched his future and his happiness walk away. It roughened his voice as he called out after her, "I dare you to come back here and work things out!"

Katie kept on walking, tears stinging her eyes. "Not this time, Nick."

TWELVE

"Mr. Leone?"

Nick spun around and glared at the sweating deliveryman who had stuck his head inside the screen door of the kitchen. As if Nick didn't have enough on his mind already—a heat wave, a temperamental new air conditioner, advertising, the health inspector, the sign maker, Katie dumping him. Katie. Pain spurred his anger. He vented it on the deliveryman. "What the hell do you want?"

"To deliver your veal," the man said in a slow, steady drawl that suddenly got on Nick's nerves. Didn't people in the South ever get rattled? Didn't they ever want to scream and throw things? The man held out a clipboard of receipts and a ballpoint pen. "You planning on cooking this meat, or do y'all just eat it raw where you're from?"

"Smart-ass," Nick grumbled as he went to open the walk-in freezer.

He knew he was supposed to be building a rapport with his delivery people. Every friendly connection was helpful in the restaurant business. Under normal circumstances he would have been cracking jokes and offering the man a cold drink. But circumstances hadn't been normal for four days.

Never in his worst nightmares had Nick imagined he could hurt so badly. Losing Katie had been like losing a vital part of himself. It was like having his heart ripped right out of his chest. He'd never been so miserable or cared less about what was going on around him. The opening of his restaurant was only days away. It was a dream coming true. It meant nothing to him if he couldn't share it with Katie.

He slumped down on a stool at the worktable and rested his elbows on the smooth new butcher block, his fingers ravaging his black hair. Couldn't she see she'd done the worst possible thing for both of them? Didn't she understand the kind of love they shared was so rare, so precious, most people went through their entire lives only dreaming about it?

Yes, he thought, she did know, and it was part of the problem. If she had loved him less, she wouldn't have felt the need to let him go.

Restless, he got up to pace around the kitchen. Love wasn't the problem. The real problem was Katie's fear of the unknown, her unwillingness to compromise, and her unwillingness to see he could compromise. Hell, he had to lay some of the blame at his own feet as well. Maybe he was at fault for his stubborn insistence on compromise. Maybe he'd pushed her too hard. He had wanted Katie and a family. Now he would have neither.

Anger and frustration rolled and built inside him until he felt as if he were a pot about to boil over. Snarling a curse he snatched up the first handy thing he could find—a copper saucepan— and hurled it across the room with all his might.

Maggie walked in as the pan crashed against the stainless-steel door of the freezer, the iron handle creasing a sharp dent in the door before the pot clattered to the linoleum.

"It's too hot for a suit of armor, Nick. Tell me I'm not going to need one."

"Come on in, Maggie," he said, going to the refrigerator. He refused to feel embarrassed for venting his emotions, especially in front of a friend. "You want a spritzer or a beer or something?"

Waving a cheap palmetto-leaf fan in her face, Maggie planted herself on the stool he'd abandoned earlier. "Anything, as long as it's tall and cold."

When he'd poured Maggie's wine cooler into an ice-filled glass and helped himself to a beer, he pulled up another stool across the worktable from her and straddled it. He raised his gold can in a brief salute before pouring a long drink down his throat.

Maggie sipped her drink and nibbled on a piece of ice, her eyes taking in every aspect of Nick's appearance. "I'd ask how you're doing, but the answer is self-evident."

It would have been pointless to deny he felt as

bad as he looked. His eyes were as bloodshot as if a night's sleep were completely foreign to him.

"I'd say Katie is about as bad off as you are," Maggie said. "It's hard to tell with her though. She's had too much practice covering up what she feels."

The mere thought that Katie was suffering tore at his gut. It brought on another surge of anger as well. "Yeah, so we're both miserable and all for no reason."

"Katie believes there's a reason."

"Well, I've got a news flash for her: She's wrong. The infallible Katie Quaid is wrong, and she's too damn stubborn to see it."

"Is she wrong, Nick?" Maggie asked gently. "You asked her to compromise. What if she can't? Do you love her enough to accept that?"

He'd asked himself the same hard question every long, lonely night since their breakup. His answer was always the same: He wanted children, but he wanted Katie more. "Yes," he answered softly.

Taking a last sip of her drink, Maggie slid off the stool and took up her fan again. She fanned herself lazily, giving Nick a long, considering look with her head tipped and her lips pursed. "Then you'd just better convince her, Yankee."

"How?" he asked as if her order were as ludicrous as telling him to try to ride to Venus on the back of a donkey.

Maggie tapped her fan against his shoulder on her way to the door. "By being just as damn stubborn as she is. Katie loves you, Nick. Don't give up on her. All the things she's wanted most in life have slipped out of her reach. Make her believe that won't happen with you."

"I'm not going."

"You're going if I have to toss you over my shoulder and carry you."

"My brother, the caveman," Katie said with a sharp edge of sarcasm in her voice. "This is the twentieth century, Rylan. You can't force a woman to go to the opening of a restaurant."

His smoky eyes narrowed and glittered. His threat was silky-soft, which made it all the more dangerous. "Watch me."

Katie's gaze roamed restlessly around her room as she reined in the urge to scream in frustration.

She crossed her arms to keep from pounding her fists against her brother's massive chest.

"Why are you so set on forcing me into going?" she asked. "Are you planning to get some sadistic kick out of watching Nick and me suffer through the evening? Don't you think he has enough to worry about without having to see me there?"

Without a word Ry went to Katie's dresser and lifted her invitation to Nick's special pre-grand-opening dinner.

"So he invited me," she said defensively. "That doesn't mean he expects me to show up. In fact, I'm sure he doesn't."

He dropped the invitation back to its place next to a bottle of French perfume and an old framed photograph of their father. He dipped his hands into the pockets of his jeans and drawled, "Yeah, I guess he probably doesn't. You've been dodging him for nearly two weeks. Why should he expect you to come out of hiding tonight?"

Katie glared at her brother. "I haven't been hiding."

He snorted derisively and uttered a raw two-syllable opinion.

"I've been avoiding him," Katie continued, undaunted by Ry's rough language, "because I think it's best. The sooner he realizes I'm not going to change my mind, the sooner he can get on with his life."

"How noble," he said with a sneer. "And convenient too."

"I don't need your sarcasm, Rylan."

"Well, you sure as hell need something," he said angrily. "You're throwing away happiness with both hands. What the hell's the matter with you, Kathryn?"

She gave him a long, level look. "Do you want the entire list?"

"Don't play the martyr with me, Katie. Self-pity doesn't become you."

It stung, but she imagined she deserved the remark at least as much as she deserved to feel the way she was feeling. "I think I have a right to feel a little sorry for myself. I had to let the man I love go—"

"And whose fault is that?"

"I did what was best for Nick."

"Oh, really? Care to explain to me then why the guy is so miserable it makes me hurt just to look at him? I've seen things lying dead along the road that look better than he does."

She didn't enjoy hearing that Nick was in pain, that he was suffering because of her. Nevertheless, she scarcely met anyone in town these days who didn't tell her so. While only Maggie and Ry knew all the details, all of Briarwood knew of the breakup; and rumors were running rampant. The general consensus was that Katie had discovered the truth about Nick's background as a spy/thief/mercenary, and she had broken up with him because of it. Sympathy, however, was running in Nick's direction, because he had become very popular around town.

Turning away from her brother, Katie stared at the floor, trying to ignore the pang of doubt. She didn't like to see Nick suffer either, but she had let him go to save him from even bigger hurt, she told herself yet again.

"He'll get over it," she said in a low, hoarse voice. "In the long run he'll see I did him a favor."

"No, Katie," Ry insisted. "I'll tell you what he sees. He sees the same thing I do. He sees you taking a walk out of his life for no reason other than you're afraid."

Why couldn't anyone understand? She wasn't the villain. She was only trying to do what was right. She was only trying to give Nick a chance to have everything he deserved. A wave of emotional exhaustion swept over her, carrying her closer to tears than she wanted to be.

"Tell me this," Ry said. "If things were different, would you marry him?"

"He hasn't asked me to marry him."

"Would you?" he asked impatiently.

Katie sighed and shook her head. "Yes. But things aren't different. I can't give him what he needs, Ry. You tell me why he should settle for less."

"Because he loves you," he said simply.

And she loved Nick. She loved him so much she ached with it. She hadn't imagined anything could hurt the way missing him did. "I couldn't live with forcing him to accept less than he deserves. I can accept my own limitations, but—"

Ry expressed his disbelief with a barnyard curse. "If you had accepted your limitations, we wouldn't be having this conversation."

Katie stepped back from him, the word betrayal written all over her face. Ry knew how hard she had fought her way back from her accident. How could he say such a hurtful thing to her? "You, of all people, should know—"

"I do know, honey," he interrupted, his harsh scowl softening along with the tone of his voice. "I know I practically had to keep you prisoner at the farm after your accident, or you would have run away from that loss too. Anyone who'd care to look can see you've built up a nice, safe little world where you don't have to face the things you think you can never have."

The words stung despite their delivery. Anger welled up inside her, making her wish she were big enough and strong enough to throw him out of her house. Unable to lash out physically, she did the next worst thing. "How dare you preach to me about hiding? How many years have you spent hiding out on the farm like some kind of hermit?"

Ry took it on the chin, but Katie caught the brief flicker of hurt in his eyes, and instantly was sorry. Ry had endured more than his share of loss and disappointment. Pressing her fingertips to her temples she hung her head and sighed. "I'm sorry."

Ry brushed her hair back from her face with his big, callous hands and pulled his sister into his arms.

"No. You're right," he murmured. "I've made mistakes. I just don't want to see you make this one, princess. Nick loves you. You love him. You're not doing him or yourself any favor by breaking it off. Don't be afraid to try for happiness with him just because you've had other things you wanted snatched away from you, Katie."

He gave her a hug that barely hinted at his strength but still managed to force the breath out of her lungs. "I'll pick you up at seven. You'd damn well better be dressed, or I'll take you there in your underwear."

Katie managed an absent smile at his final threat, but she didn't turn to watch him leave her room. When she heard the front door close, she sank down on her bed and stared across the room at her reflection in the cheval glass. The woman who stared back at her was pale, with dark smudges under her eyes and a wide mouth that turned down too easily. The last two weeks had been worse than anything she'd had to endure in five years. The strain was showing physically and emotionally.

For four days after the picnic she'd heard nothing from Nick. A part of her had been glad, had hoped he'd simply accepted her decision. A part of her had mourned both his silence and the loss of him. On the fifth day he had launched his campaign.

Gifts had begun arriving—two and three a day. Katie had sent each back to him unopened. Not that she had needed to open them to know what was in each prettily wrapped box. Everyone in town knew what Nick was up to. He even had been asking people for gift suggestions. His battle to get her back had become the hottest topic in Briarwood, far outdoing speculation as to who and what Nick Leone was or had been.

He had begun phoning her. She had refused to take his calls at the store and had unplugged her phone at home. Several times he had come into Primarily Paper to try to talk to her. She had forced herself to be coldly polite, even though it tore her up inside to treat Nick that way.

One evening he'd come to her house and tried to talk to her through the doors and windows, because she wouldn't let him in. Peter Ramsey had shown up and told him he had to leave or get hauled in for disturbing the peace.

She hadn't heard from Nick since then—two nights ago. She couldn't help but wonder if he thought she'd called Peter herself. It probably was just as well he did think so. The sooner he gave up on her the better off he'd be.

It would have been best for her to stay away from Nick's special dinner, but she would go. Katie knew she didn't have the corner on the stubborn market in the Quaid family. If Rylan believed she should be at the dinner, he would indeed carry her to it kicking and screaming.

Reluctantly she pushed herself off the bed and went to her closet to pick out a dress. She deliberately tried to empty her mind of Ry's argument, but the memory proved as stubborn as the man himself.

Ry thought she had ended the relationship because of her own fears. That wasn't true...was it? No. A sliver of uncertainty wedged itself into her mind. She tried to ignore it. If Ry was right, then she'd been fooling herself for a very long time. He was saying she was the one thing she had always fought not to be—a coward. She couldn't believe him. She had made her decision for Nick's sake . . . hadn't she? Yes.

Then why was it she suddenly felt as if a final layer had been peeled back from her soul and the real truth revealed?

Nick tried once again to tie a decent knot in his necktie. He stared at his reflection in the little mirror on the wall in his office and wondered if it was possible for fingers to develop dyslexia.

"Turn around and let me do that," his waitress, Mavis Davies, ordered. "I've tied more neckties than you'll ever see. Of course, you might be able to see the one you're wearing a little better if you'd wear your glasses." Knotting the dark green tie with sure hands, she clucked and muttered half under her breath, "You must have given your poor mama fits."

"I was a model child," he said, trying to lighten his own mood. "I was an altar boy at St. Vincent's."

"Then you'd better have St. Vincent pray for you, because I've never seen anyone so nervous."

Nervous didn't begin to cover it, Nick thought

as he took one last look in the mirror. In all his years of dancing he'd never had a case of stage fright that even came close to what he was feeling now.

Mavis gave him a motherly look from the doorway of the office. "Everything is going to go fine. The food smells wonderful, and your staff is topnotch. What is there to worry about?"

What was there to worry about? Whether or not Katie would show up. If she did show up, how would she react to the little surprises he had planned for her? He was going way out on a limb, considering she hadn't accepted any of the gifts he'd sent her, hadn't accepted any of his phone calls. He still wasn't so sure she hadn't called the cops on him the night he'd gone to see her at her house.

He had his spies though. He knew she was hurting just as much as he was. He knew she had doubts about the decision she'd made on his behalf. He knew she loved him.

What he didn't know was whether or not she was ready to give in, to give up her stubborn resolve to set him free. He had to hope she was, because he was ready to play his ace. More than once he had berated Katie for thinking in terms of all or nothing. Tonight that was exactly what he was going for—all or nothing.

Before he stepped out of his office and into the kitchen, Nick cast his gaze heavenward. "Hey, St. Vincent, put in a good word for me, will you?"

Nick's Restaurant looked exactly as Katie had pictured it, exactly as she had sketched it way back when Nick had first asked her to do the interior design. The dining room was simple but elegant with its white walls and long hunter-green drapes. The walls were lined with the old hats and walking sticks and store displays Nick had discovered in the attic. They created a wonderful, dapper, masculine atmosphere. It was perfect.

She felt her heart swell with pride for Nick. He'd worked so hard. She could remember how the place had looked the day Maggie had goaded her into checking out the mysterious new man in town.

Katie felt every eye in the room on her as she entered. She knew everyone present. Nick had planned the evening as the run-through for the staff, a trial run before the restaurant officially opened. He had invited all his new friends, who were also friends of hers. Like everyone else in Briarwood, they were well aware of the change in circumstances between her and Nick.

As she followed Ry and Maggie to the table where the Baylors sat, Katie wondered how she was ever going to be able to eat a bite of food. What was Nick going to think when he saw her? Would he be able to see how much she still loved him? Would he see the second thoughts she was having about her decision to give him up? Or had he decided by now to finally give up on her? Her friends chatted around her while she sat staring at her silverware.

The kitchen door swung open, and Katie looked up into Nick's face as he crossed the room. She felt as if her heart and her stomach were all wound up into one big knot. Nick's gaze never wavered from her face. He looked wonderful. And terrible—tired and thinner but so handsome in pleated black trousers and a crisp white shirt. She wondered if he knew the tie he was wearing was dark green.

"Katie," he said softly, handing her a menu. He

set a small basket of dinner rolls near her plate. It was all he could do to keep from scooping her up into his arms. She looked so small and vulnerable. "I wasn't sure you'd come."

She offered him a hesitant smile. "I hear the food here is pretty good."

A hint of his crooked grin moved his lips, and Katie felt her heart roll over.

He had a feeling—and wanted to believe—food wasn't the only reason she'd shown up. He'd find out one way or the other soon enough, he told himself as he forced his legs to carry him back to the kitchen, knowing Katie's gaze followed him every step of the way.

"I'll have one of everything," Ry said, perusing his menu.

Maggie frowned at him.

"Everything sounds delicious," Zoe said. "What would you recommend, Katie?"

Katie opened her menu. The list included all of Nick's specialties—*petto di pollo al champagne, arrosto di vitello*, fresh brook trout *sauté meuniere*. Before she could make a recommendation, however, an evening special caught her eye. It was carefully printed on a separate card and attached to her menu with a paper clip.

> Nick Leone's Heart on a Platter
> Softhearted Italian restaurateur
> Very much in love with you
> Will stay with you forever on your terms

Katie's eyes brimmed with tears. She knew people were staring at her, but she was beyond caring. The flood of emotions and questions and fears swirled around in her head until she felt dizzy. She needed a minute alone to catch her suddenly scarce breath and to try to calm her sudden sense of panic.

"Excuse me for just a minute, will you?" she said to no one in particular. She nearly trampled a waitress on her way to the ladies' room.

Maggie started to go after her, but Ry caught her wrist. "Let her be alone for a few minutes," he said. "Maybe she'll figure out once and for all she doesn't want to stay that way for the rest of her life."

While Maggie and Zoe discussed the wisdom of leaving Katie alone, Ry eyed the basket of rolls at one end of the table, then reached instead for one out of the basket near Katie's plate. Without bothering to tear it in two he sank his teeth into the small golden roll.

"Ouch!"

The women broke off their conversation to stare at Rylan as he examined a small diamond ring.

"Damnation! Would you look at this?" He held the tiny ring up between his thumb and forefinger. The soft light in the room turned the diamond into a prism of brilliant color. Ry scowled at it. "Jeepers cripes, I could've chipped a tooth!"

Maggie smacked his arm. "You idiot!" she said under her breath. "That's for Katie."

"What the Sam Hill was it doin' in a dinner roll then?"

"She was supposed to tear the roll open and find the ring. It's romantic, you big moron."

"What am I supposed to do with it now?"

"Put it somewhere else she'll find it by accident, and be quick about it—here she comes."

He dropped the ring into Katie's water glass, then sat back quickly.

Zoe reached out and touched Katie's arm as she sat down. "Are you all right?"

Managing to smile she nodded as she glanced around at the other dinner guests. "I'm fine."

She was anything but fine. She didn't feel any steadier now than she had when she'd read her special menu item. What was she supposed to do? She had been certain of her motives for breaking up with Nick. Now she didn't know what to think. She wanted him back, but what if that wasn't the right thing? All her life she'd been sure of herself, of her decisions. Now she couldn't even pick out what she wanted for dinner without having second thoughts.

Nearly beside herself with nerves she reached for her water glass and lifted it to her lips, only to have it yanked away from her. Water sloshed onto the dark green tablecloth.

"Rylan, what on earth?" She stared at her brother as he stuck two fingers into her glass of water and dug out a diamond ring.

"Criminey, would you look at this?" His voice boomed across the dining room as he held up the ring. He turned toward the kitchen and bellowed, "Hey, Leone, get on out here!"

Nick emerged from the kitchen, concern knitting his brows. Then he caught sight of the flash of light off the diamond, and his stomach did a free fall to his knees.

Ry stuck the ring in Nick's face. "Just look at that. Just look at what *somehow* got into my sister's glass of water. Gosh almighty, she could have choked. What do you make of it?"

Nick stared at the ring and tried to swallow down the ball of sandpaper that seemed to be lodged in his throat. Every person in the room was staring directly at him. He'd never felt as naked when he'd been working as a stripper.

"Ah—gee—ah—it looks like an engagement ring," he stammered. What the hell had happened? he wondered. The plan had been for Katie to read the note in the menu, find the ring, and then, after dinner—when all the other guests were gone—they would talk, and she would give him her answer. He sure as hell hadn't planned on proposing to her in front of half the town. What was he supposed to do now?

Ry pressed the ring into Nick's hand and made the decision for him. "Hadn't you better get down on one knee?"

It sounded like the only logical thing to do, since he didn't think his legs were going to hold him up much longer anyway. He dropped to one knee beside Katie's chair and took her limp hand in his. She stared down at him, looking utterly stunned by the turn of events. He took a deep breath and focused only on her.

"Katie, I love you. I've been so lost without you, so empty. Nothing in my life has meaning if I can't share it with you." He tugged his lower lip between his teeth for an instant, never taking his sincere, dark gaze from her face. "I want you to be my wife."

"Oh, Nick," she whispered. The rest of the people in the room faded from her view. There was only Nick. "I don't know. I don't know what to do. I love you so much, but I don't know what the right thing is anymore. I don't want to hurt you."

"Being away from you hurts me. I told you once, if I don't have you, I don't have anything. You're the woman I want to spend the rest of my life with, Katie. Everything else I'm willing to compromise on but not that. I need you."

With her free hand, she tried to brush away the

tears that clung to her lashes. "I want you to be happy. I want you to have a family, but I'm just not sure I can—"

He lifted two fingers to her trembling lips. "Shhhh. We can work it out. Together. If you decide you can't make a compromise, I can live with that—"

"But—"

He silenced her again. "Listen to me. When you let me go because you thought it was best for me, that was an act of unselfish love. Do you think I'm not capable of loving you so unselfishly as to give up something that's important to me?

"I know you're afraid, kitten. And I can't make guarantees. You know as well as I do, life doesn't come with a guarantee. But I can promise you one thing: No one will ever love you the way I do."

His words were no more than the truth, no less than her heart had longed to hear. She looked down into Nick's dark eyes and handsome face, and knew with a certainty that went soul deep, she would never love any other man the way she loved him, she would never again have the chance at happiness he was offering her now.

"Do you love me, Katie?" he asked softly.

"With all my heart."

"Do you trust me?"

"With my life."

"Will you marry me?"

"Yes," she whispered.

The next instant he was on his feet and she was in his arms, exactly where she wanted to stay for the next fifty or sixty years.

"Are you sure?" he asked.

"Yes, I'm sure. Rumor has it you're a pretty neat guy. I'd be the world's biggest fool to let you go."

The sounds of women sniffling and men clearing their throats penetrated their little world. From the corner of her eye Katie could see a lot of familiar faces staring at them with soft expressions and gentle smiles.

Nick brushed stray tears from her cheek with the pad of his thumb and smiled his crooked smile. "I dare you to kiss me in front of all these people."

With a reckless grin she raised up on tiptoe and wrapped her arms around his neck. "You're on, Yankee."

ABOUT THE AUTHOR

TAMI HOAG'S novels have appeared regularly on national bestseller lists since the publication of her first book in 1988. She lives in Los Angeles.